INCANTATIONS
AND OTHER
STORIES

INCANTATIONS
AND OTHER
STORIES

——————— ◆ ———————

ANJANA APPACHANA

Rutgers University Press
New Brunswick, New Jersey

First published in cloth and paperback in the United States of America by
Rutgers University Press, 1992

First published in cloth and paperback in the United Kingdom by Virago Press
Limited, 1991

The poem 'Sympathy', reproduced in 'Sharmaji and the Diwali Sweets' is
copyright © Paul Lawrence Dunbar; the poem 'Culture' is copyright © Edward
Bond.

Grateful acknowledgement is made to the following anthologies and journals
in which these stories first appeared: *The O. Henry Festival Stories* for 'Her
Mother'; *Eve's Weekly* and *The Forbidden Stitch, An Asian American Women's
Anthology* for 'My Only Gods'; *Room of One's Own* for 'Bahu'; *The Long
Story* for 'Sharmaji'; *The Artful Dodge* for 'Sharmji and the Diwali Sweets';
Namaste and *The Webster Review* for 'When Anklets Tinkle'; and *Imprint* for
'The Prophecy'.

Library of Congress Cataloging-in-Publication Data

Appachana, Anjana
    Incantations and other stories / Anjana Appachana.
    p. cm.
    ISBN 0-8135-1827-X (cloth) ISBN 0-8135-1828-8 (paper)
    1. India--Fiction. I. Title
PS3551.P54I53 1992
813' .54--dc20
                                        92-4708
                                        CIP

For my parents, Parvathy Appachana and S. T. Appachana,
who have always anticipated my interests,
for my husband, Rajiv, for my daughter, Malavika,
and for Penn State

Contents

◆

INCANTATIONS
AND OTHER
STORIES

My Only Gods

◆

I was four then, but some memories are still vivid, etched in my mind, like the red bougainvillaea by my grandparents' house. The colours, everywhere the colours; outside in the garden, inside, bursting forth from vases in every room. My mother's embroidery all over the house, brilliant hues of red and gold and green, like the sarees she wore. Memories of fog and fireflies, and Ponni in her purple frock . . . her lice . . . my lice. Smell of firewood drifting from the bathroom to the kitchen, mingling with the smell of meat curry. Yes, meat curry and my tantrum, the Queen of all Tantrums.

My mother and I were living with her parents. More than a year, she tells me now. My father, a distant but beloved figure, was away. He was always away, she says. We hardly saw him those years. Papa. My Papa. Who tossed me up in the air, again and again, made me fly. Who, in his green uniform and maroon beret, was the handsomest man in the world. Who took me for walks and told me the names of all the different flowers and trees. From whom I learnt, at age two, to recognise and say, pottilocus, with aplomb. To whom, held in my mother's arms, I was always waving goodbye. For my father was in the army.

Where we lived, it was always raining and I remember the sound of the rain that night, as my mother told me my bedtime story. She alternated between the *Ramayana* and children's stories. That night it was Peter Rabbit's turn. Mother Rabbit cautioned her babies not to wander into Mr McGregor's garden. Remember the end of your father, she says, Mr McGregor put him in a pie. At this point my mother began to laugh. I asked, why are you

1

laughing? Because, she replied, they made Papa Rabbit into a pie. What is a pie, I asked? (I did not know English then.) My mother struggled to find an Indian equivalent. At last she said, meat curry, my Rani, Mr McGregor made Papa Rabbit into meat curry and ate him up. And so Mama Rabbit doesn't want her babies to wander into his garden. She began laughing again.

Meat curry? Papa Rabbit cut up into little pieces? Brown bits of Papa Rabbit floating in thick gravy, gone forever? Leaving them behind, never to return? I caught hold of my mother's saree with one hand and began pounding her thighs with the other. Tears coursed down my cheeks as I screamed, don't laugh, don't laugh, don't laugh. But she couldn't stop and I threw myself on the floor, screaming and kicking my legs in a fury of anger and anguish. What's the matter with you, said my mother, trying to raise me, but I resisted and screamed louder. She picked me up and dumped me on the bed. Quiet, she said, quiet. Papa, I screamed, *my* papa. If someone made *him* into meat curry and ate him, would you laugh, would you laugh? My mother's expression changed and she wiped my tears. No one will do that, she said. I shouted, will you laugh *then*, will you laugh *then*? She hugged me. I quietened down, but stiffened as I felt her body shaking with laughter. I pushed her away, and, screaming again, threw myself on to the floor.

My tantrum lasted an hour. My grandfather smacked my bottom and I kicked him, my grandmother cajoled me with sweets and I threw them away, my mother tried to kiss me and I spurned her. It was one of my few tantrums on my father's behalf that left them all exhausted. When, finally, it was over, I sat quietly hiccupping on the floor and my mother apologised to me for having laughed. Looking suspiciously at her face, I saw no trace of amusement there, and accepted her apology. Forgiven, she went through our nightly ritual of telling me how much she loved me – more than she loved my father, more than she loved my grand-parents, more than she loved even God whom she knew so well.

Yes, my mother knew God. They were in constant touch. When I lied she would look into my eyes, then declare, you're lying. Broken, I would say, you know? And she would reply, God told me. God told her everything. When I spoke the truth, He told her it was the truth. I was sure my mother was conspiring with the Gods in my grandparents' room, which had all their photographs and images. Were they all in league with her – Lord Rama, Lord Krishna, Lord Shiva, Lord Venkateshwara, Goddess Parvati, Goddess Saraswati, Goddess Lakshmi? I suspected it was Lord Rama who told my mother, for it was Him she prayed to, His stories she told me every night. Or maybe it was Rama's devotee, Lord Hanuman. The more I pondered, the surer I was that it was Hanuman. Hanuman was a mischief-maker, had created wonderful trouble against Rama's enemy, Ravana, raided his orchards, burnt his kingdom. How I laughed when my mother told me about his escapades, how I adored him for his loyalty to Rama. When I prayed to Hanuman on Tuesdays, at the little temple outside our house, I placed extra hibiscus flowers at his feet in the hope that he would refrain from carrying tales to my mother. To no avail. My only friend, four-year-old Bina, refused to believe me when I told her of my mother's relationship with God. A box of matches tucked into her pinafore, she urged me to come with her to the end of the driveway where we could, one by one, burn them all. My hands itched with desire but my mother had once caught us at this activity and sternly forbidden it. God will tell her, I whispered to Bina. No He won't, she said, and taking my hand, led me to the end of the curving driveway. The house was out of sight. We spent ten blissful minutes taking turns striking the matches against the box, watching them burst into flame and throwing them to the ground where they slowly burnt out. Then, hand in hand, we walked back to the house and sat in the veranda. Soon my mother emerged with milk and cake. So, she said, placing them on the table, you have been playing with matches again? Bina's mouth fell open. I shook my head dumbly. Look into my eyes, my mother commanded, and, gazing deep into them, said, God tells me you're lying. Don't do it again. She left, and Bina, wide-eyed, said, it's true. Yes, I replied, triumph struggling with frustration, it's true.

I loved my mother passionately, obsessively, jealously. I was well behaved only so long as no one made overtures to her, or to me. She was careful not to show anyone affection in my presence. On the rare occasions she slipped – kissed a sister, hugged a friend – the house resounded with my screams. Fond gestures that came my way were met with immediate, unequivocal rejection. My mother warned as many people as she could, but there were always

3

those who didn't know, and suffered. One such woman, after a singularly unpleasant rejection of her advances, said of me, she has all her family's arrogance and nothing of their beauty. This was promptly conveyed to my mother who tells me how it made her seethe, all the more because she knew it was indefensible. Yes, I had none of the family's beauty, was actually almost ugly, and quite oblivious to the fact. Flat nose, huge nostrils, practically no eyebrows, a wide forehead, ears that stuck out and an expression of such pugnacity that most people kept their distance. Next to my parents I looked an anomaly, for they were both exceptionally good-looking. I was a late child, born after ten years of their marriage. During my mother's pregnancy, everybody predicted that I would be a beauty. Then I was born and they perceived that I was not, was in fact, quite the opposite. But, says my mother, they were all quite polite about it, said you were a healthy child.

How I loved her. Every night and every morning she told me how much she loved me, a ritual I never tired of. And if an ugly child could be said to bloom, at each such declaration of her love, I bloomed. Her bedtime stories filled me with delight for they were mostly about mothers and children and she would demonstrate how much the mother loved the child by kissing and cuddling me. It was my mother who made all my dresses and sweaters and when people would compliment me on what I wore, I acknowledged the compliments unsmilingly. They were only giving my mother her due, and I would only smile for her. Why was I so insatiable? She could not have possibly given me more than she did. But I wanted more more more. When the dishes were cleared after our meals, I would insist that my plate be placed over hers. Once, as I suspiciously watched the plates being stacked, my grandfather's plate was placed over my mother's. It could not be borne, and neither, says my mother, could the tantrum that followed. On the days that she washed her hair, I found the separation unbearable and waited outside the bathroom to ascertain that she came out. When I could no longer contain myself I would shout through the keyhole, Ma, call me your Rani, and she would respond, my Rani, my own Rani. Ma, call me your darling. Darling, my own darling. *Properly*, Ma, *properly. My* darling, *my* Rani. And then the endearments would become briefer and briefer as my mother lathered her hair, mixed the hot water from the big drum with the cold water in the bucket. I heard the sounds of water being poured, and waited. Then at last, Rani, I've finished, and I knew the worst was over.

We wrote to my father every day. My mother filled pages to which I added a few lines in exactly the way she did, the same round squiggles, the same periodic dots. And every day the postman delivered my father's letter. My mother gave me the envelope and read the letter over and over. Once when she had torn up my father's envelope, I had a prolonged tantrum.

My grandparents I liked. I had been made to understand that my mother was to them what I was to my mother and father. It did not seem possible though, for they had grey hair and wrinkles, belched and snored, smelled of snuff and incense, had eight other children and never told my mother stories or cuddled her. They didn't even want her on their laps. Once I insisted my mother sit on her mother's lap. My mother did, very gingerly, my grandmother groaned softly, and then they looked pleadingly at me. No, their relationship made no sense. My grandfather was delighted with this tableau, pinched my cheeks and said that I wasn't so bad after all.

And Ponni, the servant girl, three times my age, Ponni of the purple frock, Ponni with the lice. I passionately desired the frock, got the lice instead. Ponni, my companion, playmate, instructor. While my mother told me her nightly tales of the *Ramayana*, and *Little Red Riding Hood*, Ponni informed me that newly married couples *had* to sleep together without clothes. My newly married Aunt came to visit with her husband, and in a room full of chattering, excited relatives, I shook an admonishing finger at her. I said, I know what you have done. Oh, Ponni, Ponni, they sent you away, I never got to wear your purple frock and the delousing was painful.

And like the rain, the people descended. Everyone wanted to visit my grandparents. They ate up all my cake, took my mother away from me, filled the house with talk. In the summer, which was the wedding season, it was worse – a torrent of daughters, sons, grandchildren from far off cities, many related to us, came to our town, and all came home. They brought with them cards, wedding cards, printed in gold, with Lord Ganesh or Goddess

Lakshmi at the top, also in gold, with the promise of more glitter, more colour.

And one dark evening when the hills could not be seen for the fog and the fireflies were dancing beneath the big tree, he came. A distant cousin of my mother, it was his first trip in years to our little town. I had never seen anyone so tall, with eyes that danced and laughed and were the colour of ash, brown hair that glinted when the light touched it. After dinner we sat in the drawing-room and I stared unblinkingly at him. He fished into his pocket, took out a wedding invitation and tossed it on the table. For you, he told me, I want you to come for my wedding. I picked up the card and ran my finger over it. The gold print left gold dust on my fingertip. Nice. To my mind all worthwhile wedding cards did that. My mother murmured, she's not a very friendly child. He raised his eyebrows and surveyed me through his laughing eyes. Will you come for my wedding? I nodded. I would go. All those colours, beautiful women, and, best of all, the bride, like a big doll, as quiet, and exquisite in red and gold. I sat at Uncle-grey-eyes' feet and removed my socks. I said, I have red feet, and put them up for him to view. He expressed his pleasure, while my mother looked at me in shock. After showing him my red feet I somersaulted five times and told him, none of my friends can do that. He shook his head in admiration. My mother tells me, you made me feel such a fool. I wouldn't let him leave. I showed him all the sweaters my mother had knitted for me and sang two songs that Ponni had taught me. Finally, protesting, I was taken to bed by my grandmother.

After that I remember him coming often, and always, with a wedding card for me. On mornings when wedding music drifted up to our house from the samaj at the hill below, I imagined it was his wedding and urged my mother to take me. But I was told that it was still a long time away. Often in the evenings, he, my mother and I would go for walks up and down the hills. They talked a lot my mother and he, and I remember her so often, laughing. He even made me giggle – no mean achievement. Green, misty green hills, my mother's saree a brilliant yellow, he tall in grey beside her, I rolling down the hill.

I wish I could remember more. How badly I want to, for there must have been more. Or was there? I cannot remember and this,

I cannot ask her. They have filled in most of the other details of those days, all but this. But then, why should they, they didn't know, he bore no relevance to anyone but the two of us. What was he like, I wonder? Gentle, ruthless, humorous? Wicked, tender, scheming? Innocent? Handsome? I don't remember.

Because, after that, I only recall *that* day, a day filled with sunshine, when our garden was a riot of roses and the bougainvillaea, ablaze. He had come visiting again, was having coffee inside with my mother. My grandfather was asleep upstairs and my grandmother and I were in the garden, admiring the flowers. We walked up and down the driveway, talking amicably. Love for my mother filled me, could not be contained. I told my grandmother, big-big eyes, she has. Yes, she nodded. I said, long-long hair. True, she agreed, true. I said, she's *my* mother, patting my chest with my hand. Yes, said my grandmother, cutting a red rose. *Only* my mother, I said. Unable to express more, I ran towards the house to tell her how I felt.

They were in the drawing-room, she on the sofa, he on the chair opposite and there was a terrible stillness in the air. He was looking at her and she at him and I was filled with such terror that I cried out her name aloud. They started. I shrieked, go, you go. He looked at me uncomprehendingly. I jumped up and down on the carpet, my fists clenched, panting, you go, go, go, go. He got up and came towards me. I lowered my head, charged and butted him hard below his knee. I heard him take in his breath and felt my mother's fingers grasping my shoulders as I lowered my head again. I didn't stop screaming till he left, escorted outside by my flustered, apologetic grandmother and sleepy, irritable grandfather.

Spoilt, awful child, my grandfather told my mother when they came in. No manners, no sense of propriety. My mother, pale in her red saree, said nothing. I glowered at him. My grandmother shook her head reprovingly. She said, such an unpredictable child. She should mix more with children her age. My grandfather bent down and told me, bad girl, waking me up with your screaming. Furiously, I replied, *you* bad boy, you snore and wake *me*. My mother said, shhh.

I remember him coming just once more, and when I saw him in the driveway I began screaming like a person possessed. He stopped, turned and walked away. I trailed my mother with renewed persistence, refused to go anywhere without her, did not allow her to go anywhere without me. My mother's daily bedtime stories became abstracted.

Then, suddenly, there were those endless days without her. My grandmother told me that she had fever and that the doctor was making her all right. I was inconsolable. I wandered from room to room, looked for her in the bathroom, in the kitchen, under the beds and in the cupboards, finally shutting myself in her wardrobe, smelling her among her sarees, her talcum powder smell. My grandmother found me there much later, holding her petticoat against my face. She tells me that she couldn't bear it, burst into tears and asked my grandfather to send a cable to my father.

And my father came. My grandmother says, you held on to him and did not let go of him that entire evening. You didn't even let him get up to eat or go to the bathroom. Your poor, patient father. That night his unfamiliar body occupied the bed I shared with my mother and I cried for her again.

And my mother came. It was just five days, you know, she tells me. The reunion was ecstatic, if dramatic. How you women wept, my grandfather says, shaking his head. You, your mother, your grandmother. All weeping. But at least this time you didn't have your famous tantrum. And, says my father, I had my posting orders by then, there would be no more separations for us. I ask, but what happened, what *was* this illness? We are sitting in the veranda in my grandparents' house, it is the summer holiday and once again, the garden is bursting with colour. Nervous breakdown, says my grandfather. What! I exclaim. Nothing serious, he says. Must be running in the family, your grandmother had one too. Lucky for you that your mother was back in just five days. My grandmother kisses her hand and places it on my cheek, saying, she was back only because of you. She couldn't live without you. I say, oh Ma, how lonely those years must have been for you. Very, she answers, very.

Must be running in the family, he said. Well, either that or the tantrum. At thirty-six you couldn't have opted for the tantrum, could you, Ma? At twenty-five, neither can I. Too old for tantrums, too old. And I managed not to have the other, came back here instead, the memory returned, they filled in the rest and the dust slowly settled. Yes, finally.

My Only Gods

There is a long silence and then my mother smiles and tells me, that night when the three of us were finally together, you put your arms around your father's legs, reached up and kissed his bottom. You said, Papa, they didn't make you into meat curry.

Bahu

◆

That day we saw our first film in months. We never had time for these things any longer. I had (foolishly) presumed that my husband and I could go together, but the entire family decided that they, too, wanted to accompany us. So in the end we were seven: my parents-in-law, sister-in-law, brother-in-law, their eight-year-old son, my husband and I. It would have been a year since we went out, just the two of us.

The film was terrible. I would have left but for the family who were glued to their chairs, the women weeping copiously at the heroine's plight. The heroine, self-effacing and self-sacrificing, was beautiful and beloved by all. A doting bahu and wife, she manages her house and her in-laws with efficiency and sweetness. In between household chores she and her husband frolic in the nearby park, sing love songs, roll down undulating hills and chase each other through a blaze of blossoming flowers and gulmohar trees. But the villain desires the heroine. Her husband and in-laws, wrongly believing that she is having an affair with him, turn her out of the house. She throws herself at their feet, but to no avail. Pregnant but forgiving, she wanders the streets of the city, finally giving birth to a baby. It's a boy, says the nurse. I knew it, she replies, I have always wanted a son. She returns with her son to her in-laws, who, in the meantime, have discovered her innocence. Once again, she flings herself at their feet and begs forgiveness for whatever wrong she may have committed. This time she is forgiven. You are my Sita, her husband says emotionally. Even the Lord Rama abandoned his pregnant wife in the forest.

At this point I told my husband that I would wait for them

10

outside the hall. I stepped out into the oppressively hot night. The rains had still not come. The monsoon was two weeks' overdue and a terrible drought was predicted if it did not arrive soon. I was drenched in sweat. How much longer could this go on? I thought of the monsoon months at home (my home, my parents' home) sitting out on the veranda with Ma and Pa, watching the rain; Ma telling me ancient stories of rain clouds bearing messages from one lover to another, Pa looking contemplatively into the distance. How long was it since I had gone home? A year. And my parents were just a fifteen-hour journey away by train. But my in-laws' servant had absconded six months ago and there was no way I could go home until we found another one. And when (if) we found another one I would probably not get leave from the office. I walked down the car park slowly. It seemed an eternity since I had talked to anyone, or anyone had talked to me. I felt so overwhelmingly homesick. Our parents give us such total, unconditional love. Why do we feel we'll always have it? I know that I always did. I began to walk back. The film would be over soon. I felt a movement behind me, a middle-aged man slid past, feeling my thigh and muttering an obscenity under his breath as he did. For the first time in my life my reflexes did not fail me. I ran after him, saree and all, hit him hard with my bag and ran back into the theatre. I stood inside, panting. He did not come after me, thank God. I had never done this before, on all those numerous occasions when these disgusting men fingered me. Either I was scared of what they would do if I retaliated or my reflexes just did not work. They think it's their prerogative. What a sick city this is. There is so much cruelty and frustration under its veneer of sophistication. Why do they do it? It wouldn't give me pleasure to feel a strange man's thighs on the road or on the bus. The DTC is a nightmare. No one does anything, often passengers or bystanders look on and laugh. Either that, or they look away. When I go back to the house and cry, people there say, you're too sensitive, other girls survive. Yes they survive, we all survive.

They came out of the theatre and my mother-in-law said, someone here only likes high-brow films, simple emotions do not appeal to her. Everyone laughed. I smiled too. I said, what simple emotions, Ammaji? She was misused, she shouldn't have gone back. My mother-in-law replied, really? But then you see, she was not like you. She was a simple girl. She did her duty. My husband gave me a warning look. We were walking back to the car. I ignored him. Ammaji, I said with a laugh, don't I do my duty? With a tight smile she said, ask yourself that question. Are you ever at home? My husband pinched my arm. We were in the car. I said, I am not at home because I have a job, Ammaji. She replied, that is your choice. No one forced you to have a job. There was dead silence in the car. My brother-in-law gave a nervous giggle. I waited for the surging in my ears to subside, then I said, Ammaji, don't I still do all the work in the house? She answered, that is your duty.

There was a longer silence, then she said, there is no need to answer me back in this fashion. Sometimes I wonder what you think of yourself. Count yourself lucky to have married into this family. How many families from our caste do not take dowry? We did not take a paisa from your parents. Our son had plenty of offers from families in our community. Yet we welcomed you with open arms. And look at you. You have no concern for our feelings, you do exactly what you want. How many bahus wear trousers in front of their in-laws? On the contrary they cover their heads in front of their elders. We have not stopped you from working. You spend your salary the way you wish. Other working bahus give their entire salaries to their mothers-in-law. Have we ever forbidden you to go to your parents for one month at a stretch? We even allow you to call our son by his name in our presence. All this is because we are liberal, enlightened. We have allowed you all these concessions. And yet you go around with a long face giving people the impression that we are beating you, ill-treating you.

Oh you do go on, groaned my father-in-law.

Now, after two years, it was out in the open. I had always known how she felt about me. Every day, for two years, I had listened to her insinuations. At last she had said it.

I was trembling. Ammaji, I said, I have not seen my parents for a year. Your own daughter has been with you for two months. Only, that was not what I meant to say. I meant to say more. I meant to say it all.

Enough, she said. I do not want to hear any more. Ammaji, I said desperately (Oh God, please let her understand), I really could do with some help in the house.

There was a stunned silence in the car.

So, said my mother-in-law, it has come to this. Next you will ask my poor son to help you in the kitchen when he comes back tired from office.

Still trembling, I looked out of the window. I could feel Siddharth's anger at my unexpected behaviour. I had to talk to him. I had to. I could not talk with her. But when?

Dinner was eaten in silence except for my father-in-law who loudly praised my cooking and urged me to make chicken curry at the week-end. My mother-in-law made a disbelieving sound.

By the time I washed the dishes and cleaned the kitchen it was well past midnight. I went to our room and found that my husband's nephew had fallen asleep on the diwan next to our bed. He's so fond of his mamaji, my sister-in-law would say each time this happened. My husband was asleep too. So, in fact, was the whole household. I could not have it out tonight. Or any other night if things continued this way and they would continue this way as long as we lived and we would live this way forever and forever.

I opened the front door and stepped out on to the veranda. Alone at last. The sky was grey and starless, everything was still and hot. I could hear the chowkidar taking his nocturnal rounds and in the distance a dog barked. I sat on the steps and began to weep. I was tired of timing my tears.

In books they speak of the moment of revelation, the sudden and overwhelming realisation of one's predicament. In fact it doesn't happen that way. There's no one moment. Each time you give in you persuade yourself that the adjustment is necessary to marriage. There's no point upsetting people when you're living with them. There won't be a next time. But there is. You give in again, and again, and again. There comes a time when it isn't such a small matter any more. But, still overwhelmed with guilt, still determined to please, you succumb again. Imperceptibly, but irrevocably, you slide into the kind of life that is completely and terribly contrary to everything you believe in. The kind of life you discussed in those pre-marital days (blissfully principled) saying, *I would never accept such a thing. I would walk out.*

Now the situation is yours. You have not walked out. You will live this way, always?

★

When Siddharth and I fell in love it really was a dream come true. I walked on clouds those days. I thought of him all the time, of his smile, his walk, his voice, his smell. I loved his kindness to people, his infinite gentleness. His gentleness disarmed me, his tenderness won me completely. He was intelligent and well read. He was what I had always dreamt of, the man who would be my friend, my companion, my lover. Mine would not be one of 'those' marriages. I saw them all around me, marriages where neither shared the other's dreams, speaking to each other only of their children, rising prices, the cost of vegetables and fruits – they never spoke of each other. The women, they endured, they had much to endure. Like my mother. Only my sisters and I knew my mother's anguish, all those frustrations, years and years of it. My father was oblivious to her pain for he was oblivious to its causes. She never spoke of it to him, and he would never have understood. I suppose in his own way he loved her, he certainly could not have done without her. He would never know that my mother had dreams other than those of being a good wife and mother. She realised some of her dreams through us, her three daughters. With his daughters, my father was different. He spent time with us, encouraged us in all our different interests and in all that we wanted to do. But not with my mother.

With Siddharth *my* dreams seemed possible. What days! The Delhi summer played havoc with our passions – its water shortage, power cuts and unrelenting heat left us after work, washed out, hot, drenched with sweat and longing. We must have spent hours gazing passionately, desperately and quite helplessly at each other across endless cups of tea and coffee. We both lived with our parents, there was no place to go. Once in a park we held hands and were soon followed by a group of young men singing songs.

After marriage, I thought, it will be different. Time at last to be together.

A few days before our wedding I discovered that my parents were spending 15,000 rupees on gifts for Siddharth, his parents, sister, brother-in-law, nephew, aunts and uncles. I was furious. I raged, I cried. My parents did not listen. This is between the parents, they said. You and Siddharth keep out of it. Besides, they added, his parents have not demanded any cash. Then why give all this? I asked. My mother replied, they expect it.

I spoke to Siddharth that day. I was filled with foreboding. He laughed at my fears. Don't be silly, he said. These are traditions one cannot break. Your mother is right. We should keep out of it. I said, we are the ones getting married. He replied, relax, there is nothing to get so worked up about. I said, your mother gave mine a list of your relatives to whom we should give sarees and suits. It will cost my parents 10,000 rupees. Siddharth said, well, they can afford it, can't they? I went cold. Siddharth, I said, you know that's not the point. He sighed and said, these are gifts given with great happiness on the occasion of a wedding. Take it in that spirit and stop attributing motives to it.

I tried to accept it in that spirit but could not. By his own logic, gifts given so spontaneously should be given both ways. And we both knew that there was no question of my family receiving 'gifts given with happiness' from his family. I gave in. The wedding was just a week away and I did not want to make a scene.

After my marriage I moved to my in-laws' three-bedroomed house. Soon after, my father was posted outside Delhi.

We never went for a honeymoon. My mother-in-law wanted me to spend time with the relatives who had come down for the wedding. She felt that this was the best time to get to know them and receive their blessings. Siddharth did not protest. I could not. The relatives, about twenty of them, stayed in our house, and left a couple of weeks after the wedding. Siddharth and I spent the mornings, afternoons and evenings with them. They were genuinely interested in me, wanted to know all about me, lavished affection on me. How guilty I felt for resenting them. But I did so want time alone with Siddharth, time to enjoy laughter and silences, time to discover one another. Don't be silly darling, Siddharth would tell me, it's just for another few days. I was a good bahu those days, I wore my heaviest silk sarees and jewellery and touched everyone's feet every morning.

By the time they left it was time for Siddharth and me to get back to work. With relief, I packed away the heavy silks and put away the jewellery in the locker. The days then followed a familiar pattern – to work in the morning, back in the evening, guests and relatives who visited at teatime, often staying on for dinner. My father-in-law, a great admirer of my culinary skills, would urge

15

me to cook their favourite dishes. Weekends were spent with relatives again. There were so many of them to visit, so many lunches and dinners to return, so many obligations to fulfil. I told Siddharth mournfully, we have so little time together. We never talk. He seemed surprised. We'll never have more time than this, he said, and you must spend more time with all my relatives, they are anxious to get to know you. I did spend time with them, but it was never in addition to the time spent with Siddharth, it was instead of. We never seemed to have time for my own relatives and friends.

And then, it began. My mother-in-law would sigh and say how difficult it was for her to manage the house while I was at work. Yes, the servant cooked and cleaned the house, but still, management was something else. She smiled sadly and said, I thought it would be different after you came. Gently, she said, take more care of the house after you come back from work, things are in such a mess. I could see no mess but bustled around for an hour after work. She said, at least twice or thrice a week, make a meal for us. Must we eat from the servant's hands when a new bahu has come to the house? So I did. There is no variety in the fruits and vegetables we eat, she said, when I managed the house we had something different for breakfast, lunch and dinner. I don't know what is happening these days. There was variety. She said, so much food is wasted in this house, no one seems to do any budgeting here. Her daughter came to stay for two months at a stretch. She said, there is no one to indulge my poor child, no one to cook her favourite dishes, she cannot eat from a servant's hands. Once I cooked for her. Now I am too old and it seems no one else can do it. If you are so busy, at least take her out to her favourite restaurants. We did. On the day of her daughter's fast she wept. As I stepped into the house after work, she said, my poor child is on a fast and there are no fruits for her in this house. She wiped her eyes with her saree and said, people in this house have never been stingy, always there have been fruits in the house. I don't know what is happening these days. I said, Ammaji, the fruit shop is just behind the house. She replied, so now at least get some fruits for her. She adored her grandson. She said, let him play in your room. He likes your room. There is no need to shut the door. In a large family one has to have a large heart. One has to learn to share. When I returned from a sitar recital one evening, she said, in my days a bahu was more responsible, she spent more time in the house. Spend more time in the house was to become her constant refrain. The all too rare outings we had already stopped, for her displeasure on our return would fill the house. I could not bear the homecoming. Siddharth said, if it upsets her, we won't go out. It isn't the end of the world if you don't see an art exhibition or can't play your sitar. There are other things in life. I replied, like what? The kitchen, cooking, relatives, small talk – everything but each other or our interests? He said, it doesn't bother me, you shouldn't let it bother you. I still wonder whether it really did not bother him or whether this was his way of keeping the peace. I waited for Siddharth to notice his mother's remarks. But in his presence, she said nothing. At night I would lie awake, looking at my sleeping husband, wondering, what is happening, is there something wrong with me? Ultimately I brought it up. Siddharth told me, as usual you're imagining things. I've never heard her say anything to you. I said, she never stops. He replied, oh for heaven's sake, stop exaggerating. If she does criticise you, she must have a good reason for doing so. Doesn't your own mother criticise you? I said, my mother loves me. To such outbursts he would groan, oh God, and he would turn over and fall asleep.

How I longed to see my parents. My mother-in-law did not approve. In disbelief, she said, you want to go when my daughter is here? I could not get leave from office the following month, her daughter was here for two. In that case, she said, you should take a month's leave and spend fifteen days at home with us. It doesn't seem that there is a bahu in this house, the way things are here. You have an obligation to us too. Of course, Siddharth had no obligation to my parents.

And so the days went by and my sitar gathered dust, as I listened to my sister-in-law speak of life and liberty, my brother-in-law of the need for more honest people in the country, my mother-in-law of the negative influence of western culture on Indian women. I listened while my father-in-law quoted poetry and Siddharth ranted about the weakness of the Indian people, the Indian love of authority. No one can stand up to anyone, he would say despairingly, our country is going to the dogs. It pained him that I expressed no opinions about politics. It was wrong, he said, completely wrong to be so apolitical. Doesn't what is happening in our country affect you? he would ask. Even my mother has an opinion to offer. I despair for you. They all despaired for me. I had no political beliefs, was not religious, did not pray, never fasted, had no expressed opinion on life.

Then, a year after our marriage, I became pregnant. I didn't want the baby. The implications of motherhood filled me with horror. I would be completely trapped. I would have to give up my job to look after the child and in the bargain look after everyone else. I would have no choice but to be a good bahu twenty-four hours a day. Once the child went to school I would be too long out of the job market to find another job. My in-laws were delighted. They said it would be a boy. He would resemble their Siddharth. They named him Mohan. They planned his future. They said, at least now you will give up your precious job. A child needs his mother.

It was my old friend, who, in all innocence asked me if the family observed the usual customs if a boy were born. What customs, I asked, puzzled. She giggled. The usual, she said. Your parents will have to come loaded with gifts for them. She saw my expression and touched my arm. She said, it doesn't always happen. My in-laws didn't insist, I'm sure yours won't.

I asked Siddharth. He said, I have no idea. Why must you spend all your time thinking about stupid things like this? I replied, because it's bound to come up after the baby is born, and then I'll be in no state of mind to fight about it. Siddharth gave an exclamation of disgust. He said, your misery is of your own making. You spend all your time anticipating problems. I replied, I have to, this time I have to.

I asked his mother. Smiling, I said, I'm sure you don't believe in such old-fashioned customs. She did not smile back. She said, there is nothing old-fashioned about these customs. These are long-standing traditions. When your son is born, your parents will happily give gifts to our family to celebrate the occasion. Barely able to speak, I asked, what gifts, Ammaji? She shrugged, oh well, it is up to your parents. Kanchivaram sarees to the women in the house, and suits to the men.

I mentally calculated – 12,000 rupees. I said, smiling, and what do my parents and sisters get for becoming grandparents and aunts?

My mother-in-law looked at me distrustfully. She said, sometimes your questions make no sense. The chapter was closed.

I went back to Siddharth. I said, my parents will have to spend 12,000 rupees on gifts for your family if it is a boy.

Siddharth laughed. Maybe, he said, it will be a girl. He caressed my cheek. I hope it will be a girl.

I brushed aside his hand and locked the room. I said, I want to talk to you. For once listen to me. I will not follow these customs. I won't let your family fleece mine on every so-called happy occasion. Are you listening? I couldn't believe it was my voice. I sounded hysterical, crazed.

Siddharth looked stunned. He shook his head slowly. He said, you sound like you're going crazy. I don't want to talk to you. He went towards the door.

I stood against the door with my back to it. No, I said, no. I won't let you go out until we can talk about it. You never want to talk about anything. It's time we do.

He stood there, staring at me. At last he said, what is there to talk about?

Do you agree with what your mother told me?

Whether I agree or not is immaterial. If it has to be done, it has to be done.

It doesn't have to be done.

He shrugged his shoulders. That's your headache then. He drew a deep breath and said, it doesn't take much to make my mother happy. You know she's old-fashioned. How do you expect her to think the way you do? What does it cost you to observe these traditions?

Twelve thousand rupees and everything I believe in.

Very dramatic.

There was a knock on the door. Siddharth pulled me away and opened it. It was his sister. She looked at us curiously. Amused she said, lovers' tiff, hmmmm? It happens. She came in, sat on the bed and began talking about her shopping trip.

That night I miscarried. They took me to the hospital but it was too late. For the next few days I lay in bed in the house, completely drained of strength. I felt no sorrow for the child I had lost. On the contrary I felt overwhelming relief. Siddharth stayed by me, for once, comforting. On the third day my mother-in-law came to our room and told us, my heart is breaking to see my poor daughter working in the kitchen. The poor child does not want to see her mother work. She is making chappatis with her own hands for us.

When she went out of the room I began to cry. Siddharth was horrified. I said, even now she can't stop her insinuations. If I can make chappatis, why can't she? Siddharth replied, she wasn't insinuating anything. If you weren't so unwell I'd be angry. I continued crying and Siddharth sat by me, helpless, uncomprehending, frustrated. He went back to work the next day. My mother-in-law made it clear that I should resume my responsibilities in the house. I did and I also went back to work.

Later Siddharth told me that the miscarriage was all my fault. He said, you worked yourself into that state. At this rate you'll never be able to have a baby. I replied, I don't want one. He said, I suppose you'll blame my mother for that too. I opened my mouth to reply and he stopped me. Please, he said, I'm sick of all this. If you can't adjust in our family please don't take it out on me.

That night I thought, they have assumed complete control over my life. I have let them. But what could I do? It was all so strange, so bewildering. All those new people, new relationships; sudden, unexpected do's and don'ts. Were they wrong or was I? I was overwhelmed with guilt. How was it possible for all of them to be wrong and only I right?

And Siddharth. What about Siddharth? I must accept it, mustn't I? That he let it be. He chose to let it be. He saw. How could he help but see, he was not blind. Yes, he chose to let it be.

He could have stopped it, protected me. Only he could do that. I needed protection, I needed him. I hardly knew the others. He just had to say to them, she's tired, let her rest. She's working, none of you are. She cannot cope. He could have changed it all. Instead he said, you're not spending time with the family, there's no need to spend an hour every day on your sitar. He could have said, I'll help you with the work and so will my mother and sister. Instead he said, you never smile. He could have said, I need more time with my wife. Instead he said, there's no need to be so resentful when people come to our room, you mustn't be so selfish. He could even have said, I don't know what we would have done without you. But he said, you look a wreck. But mostly he said nothing.

Had he changed? Or had he always been like this? I wasn't sure any more. At first I thought he had changed, changed terribly. It was a stranger I faced every morning, a stranger who turned his back to me every night, groaning, please stop cribbing, I'm tired. I had to talk to somebody. He didn't want to listen. Or maybe, as my long married old friend told me wisely, it was just another side to him that I was seeing. What could I have seen of it before our marriage? Then, there was no context for conflicts to arise. What indeed had he known of me? I don't recall a single argument we had before our marriage. I remember him saying that he loved me most for my sweet, calm disposition, the fact that I never spoke ill of anyone. And here I was, constantly complaining, if not every night, then at least whenever he was awake to hear me. You've become a nag, he said, and I went cold with horror. A nag. I had become a nag. My father called my mother a nag when they argued, my father-in-law called my mother-in-law one . . . I had become that? Where, oh where, was my sweet, calm disposition? I had never known that I could be so obsessively unhappy.

One day, weighed down with misery, I took leave from the office to talk to my friend. I talked, she listened. After a while she asked me, do you love him? I could not answer. She repeated, do you? I said, I did once. Now, I don't know. The realisation, till now barely acknowledged, shook me terribly. She said, it's important that you know. If he took a stand and you lived separately, would it be different for you? It was, for us. Despairingly I said, I don't know, I just don't know. He'll never do that. I can't think beyond now. She said, and what about him, does he care for you? I knew the answer and it didn't make it easier. I said, he does, in his own way he does. She waited. I said, it won't do, he doesn't want to listen. Love has nothing to do with it, nothing at all.

How distant my pre-marital days seemed. I had known independence then, had pursued all my interests, including my one passion, music. Four times a week, I went for my sitar classes. I had given two, very successful performances on stage. My parents and I attended every festival of music in the capital; those months from October to February were a delight. Indian classical music touched something in me that nothing else, no one, did. My parents understood. They did not share my passion but unfailingly accompanied me to every event I wanted to attend. I could never go on my own as it was unsafe to return unescorted at that time of the night. We did not have a car and were dependent on Delhi's undependable and often, nightmarish public transport.

At home, no one felt I had failed them (except when I refused to go in for an arranged marriage and my relatives gloomily prophesied that I would die a spinster). I contributed to the running of the house and helped my mother with the housework. Though I had less time for my interests once I started working, I did pursue them. And coming back home after work was . . . so different. It was a haven. My parents and I would sit together and chat. It was my first year at work, and I was excited by each small accomplishment, worried if things did not go as I thought they should. Sometimes we argued, mostly about my getting married. They were unhappy and worried about how vehemently I opposed it, how angry I would get every time they brought up the subject of an eligible match for me. I said, I can't live with a man I don't know. My mother said, you might never meet anyone you like. My father said, your knight in shining armour may never come. But they did not press me. After a couple of years they stopped talking about it and instead, looked unhappy. For me, life went on as usual, and if sometimes, I wondered, will it ever happen to me, I also felt that if it didn't, maybe it did not matter. I had an excellent job, I had my music, I was dependent on no one. Most importantly, I had people who loved me, who in times of stress, were always there. I recall times when I was unhappy, but never alone.

Now I was alone. There was no one I could talk to. Even if my parents had been here I would not have confided in them for they would not have stopped worrying. My closest friends no longer came to the house, for they invariably found me attending to relatives and by the time I was free it was time for them to go. With understanding and affection they said, it would be better if you come and see us at our home, we'll have time to talk. That rarely worked out. So I would phone them from the office and talk in the code language of our school days (the telephone operator would invariably be listening). The only time I had to myself was during the bus journey to work and back. I spent this time avoiding insistent thighs and moving through packed aisles to the front of the bus where there was some respite. Sometimes I was lucky to get a seat where my male companion did not press himself against me. Then I would sit for an hour, free to immerse myself in my thoughts and watch the people go by. It's strange what comfort an uncrowded bus can offer you. You drift along quite pleasantly, recall happy times, even dream a little. I would dream of Siddharth and I having a place of our own; imagine what it would be like to have all the time in the world for each other. Blissful solitude. Wonderful, wonderful independence. It could never be. Siddharth did not want it.

What did he want? Why had he married me? If it was for someone to attend to the kitchen and relatives every day of her life, someone who had to conform to all the traditional expectations of a good bahu . . . then why me?

Had he at that time known it would be like this? Probably not. He could not have known any more than I did.

But he knew now. Why then did he accept it? Had he no dreams for us?

And love . . . love . . . that's how it all began. It will never do, it will never never do.

What could I do? I had chosen this life. I had to live it. I could not change it.

I had not chosen it. No, I had never done that. I had no idea that this was what marriage to Siddharth entailed, no idea at all. How could I have possibly known? They were all highly educated. Why had I assumed that education implies enlightenment? I had taken that for granted. How could I have done otherwise? What indication had there been that their attitudes had not changed in any way? None. No, I had not chosen this.

I could not change it. I could not change the way they thought. Did they really think this way, or was it just more convenient for them to do so?

I could not change it. Especially since Siddharth accepted it. Did I then also accept it? Could I? How could I go backwards? Acceptance would mean that I would live this way, always. It would never mean that I could accept it as the right thing to do. How then could I do it, day after day, year after year. For whom? And why?

And if I could neither accept it as a way of life, my way of life, nor as what is right . . . where did it leave me? I couldn't leave them. What would I say? They wouldn't understand. What could I tell them? My mother-in-law would say, I always knew it, she is like that, it is as I expected. My father-in-law would whisper, beti, what are you doing? What have we done? I could see the light from his eyes fade.

And Siddharth, what would he say? What could I tell him? Let us live separately. On our own. He would say, why what's wrong with this house, are my parents ill-treating you? Then what would I say? Yes, they are, you all are. It cannot go on like this. I have no privacy at all, no independence. It is not my house. We have no time together. He would reply, of course we do, aren't we together after work every day? I would ask, are we, Siddharth? You watching TV, me in the kitchen? Well, he would say, I can't help that can I? I would say, oh yes, yes, you can, only you can. And would I also say, no one really cares for me, not even you Siddharth. His reply would be, you're neurotic, you're imagining things as usual. Someone would enter our room and the conversation would come to a halt. Maybe an hour later I would say, Siddharth, what kind of marriage is ours? He would reply, Oh God, there you go again, and he would go to the living-room to watch TV. I would follow him and find him with all the others. Talk to me, I would plead silently, listen to me . . . but my message would be lost and it would be time to cook dinner. After dinner the family would sit in our room and chat. An hour later I would say, Siddharth, I cannot take it any more. He would be fast asleep.

And would I then wake him up and say, I'm leaving?

Where would I go? Not to my parents. They would urge me to go back, tell me how important it is to preserve a marriage. They would say, it is not easy to be a divorced woman in India. What will people say? My mother would tell me, all said and done, it is the woman who has to give in more. You had better accept that.

Ten years from now you will be glad you took our advice. But their hearts would be breaking.

I could not leave this city. Where else could I find such a good job? I had just four years' work experience and jobs were so hard to come by. I could leave and take up a barsati somewhere, provided that someone was willing to let out one to a woman separated from her husband. I would have joined the slender bandwagon of 'those women'. No, it would not be easy to find a place. In the meantime I had my friend.

What would it be like to stay on my own? Just me and my room, my books, my music, my friends? Some men would think I was easy game. What would they say at work? 'We always thought she was such a nice girl. One wouldn't have expected this of her.

At dawn I was still sitting on the steps, spent. The rain clouds were gathering. At last. I could hear the clattering of dishes in our neighbour's kitchen. People were hurrying along with steel cans to the milk booth. Old men in their pyjama-kurtas and walking sticks were going briskly for their morning walks, determined to make it before the downpour.

Siddharth found me in the veranda and I told him that I was leaving him. He was silent for a long time. At last he asked, where will you go? I said, I'll find a place. He sat by my side on the steps. Listen, he said haltingly, I know you're tired. We'll get a servant soon. He waited for me to say something. He said, you can't go like this. How do you think it will affect my parents? He waited again. He said, you need a break. Take one after the servant comes. Go to your parents for a couple of weeks. I'm sure Amma will allow you to.

I got up. I have to pack, I said.

He caught me by the arm. Please, he said, we need to talk.

His mother came out on to the veranda. He let go of my arm. She raised her eyebrows.

Isn't the tea ready? she asked me.

No, I replied.

You make the tea today, Amma, Siddarth said. She isn't feeling well.

My mother-in-law looked at me expressively and went into the kitchen.

Siddharth followed me to the bedroom. He shut the door. His nephew was still asleep on the divan. I sat on the bed, exhausted.

Don't think I don't understand, Siddharth said. But what can be done about it? This is the way things are. You have to learn to accept it.

No, I said. I walked to the window and looked out at the overcast sky. It was going to pour.

Why not? he said. I have.

I opened the cupboard and began taking out my sarees. He came to me and turned me around. Don't go, he said. His eyes were full of pain.

Siddharth, I said —

Where are you going, Mamaji? His nephew was awake and listening. I did not reply.

Go to your room, Siddharth told him.

No, he replied, I want to stay here. Siddharth looked at him helplessly. Be a good boy and go, he said.

His nephew looked at him and then at me. His face puckered up. I want to stay, he said.

Siddharth drew a deep breath. All right, he said, but don't talk.

I began to pack.

Siddharth lowered his voice. Try and understand, he said. Abdicating your responsibilities isn't the answer.

I continued packing. They both watched me.

I was packed and ready in an hour. I did not say anything to my in-laws. I left that to Siddharth. I wondered who would make the breakfast and dinner today. I phoned my friend and told her that I would be coming over for a few days. She said that she would wait for me. I said, please take the day off from work. She replied, I will. I called a taxi. My sister-in-law and brother-in-law were still asleep. My parents-in-law said nothing. Perhaps Siddharth had told them. Perhaps they knew. I don't know. They sat on the veranda, stirring their tea, not looking at me. My father-in-law suddenly looked very old. Yes, the light from his eyes had faded. My mother-in-law had the expression that goes with the words I had imagined. Siddharth helped me load the suitcases and my sitar into the taxi. I sat inside. He put his hand over mine. He said, I'll wait for you. I shook my head. It began to rain as the taxi moved forward, and I breathed in deeply – at last, the smell of wet earth.

Sharmaji

◆

Sharma was late for work. When he signed his name in the attendance register, the clerk in the personnel department shook his head disapprovingly.

'Very bad, very bad, Sharmaji,' he said, clicking his tongue. 'This is the fourteenth time you are late this month.'

Sharma's brow darkened. 'You keep quiet, Mahesh,' he replied. 'Who are you to tell me I'm late? You are a clerk, I am a clerk. You don't have the authority to tell me anything. Understand?'

Mahesh retreated behind his desk. He said, 'What I am telling you, I am telling you for your own good. Why you must take it in the wrong spirit I do not understand.'

'You don't tell me what is good for me,' Sharma said. He raised his voice. 'I am twenty-five years older than you.'

He had an audience by now. The other latecomers and those working in the personnel department were watching with intense interest.

Sharma continued, 'I have been in this company for twenty-five years. At that time you were in your mother's womb.' He surveyed his delighted audience. 'He thinks that after reading our personal files he has power over us.' He snapped his fingers in front of Mahesh's face. 'I can show you how much power you have! What can a pipsqueak like you teach me! It is for *me* to teach *you!*'

'Sharmaji,' said Mahesh, folding his hands, 'I take back my words. Now please leave me alone. And I beg of you, do not shout in the personnel department. It sounds very bad.'

Sharma chuckled. He raised his voice. 'Shouting? I am not

shouting. I am talking to you. Is it forbidden to talk in the personnel department? Is this an office or a school?' He smiled again at his audience. Everyone was spellbound. He said, 'So Mahesh, you now think you can tell me how to behave. Very good. What else can you teach me?'

'Yes, Mahesh, tell him,' urged Gupta, the clerk from the accounts department. He was also late, but only for the ninth time in the month.

Mahesh looked harassed. 'You keep out of this, Gupta. This is not your business.'

'Mahesh,' said Gupta. 'You are in the wrong profession. You should have been a teacher, a professor. Join Delhi University. We will all give you recommendations!'

Everyone roared with laughter. Mohan, the peon, was the loudest. 'Today we are having fun,' he said between guffaws, 'Oh, this is wonderful!'

'What is wonderful, Mohan?'

It was the personnel officer, Miss Das. A sudden silence fell in the room. Everyone looked away. She glanced at her watch and then at the silent group. 'What is happening?' she asked. 'Why is there this mela here?'

'Madam, we came to sign the attendance register,' Sharma said. Gupta slid out of the room.

She looked pointedly at her watch. 'The register should have been signed forty-five minutes ago.'

Sharma looked her straight in the eyes. 'Madam,' he said, 'What to do, my daughter had temperature. I had to take her to the clinic so I got a little late.'

'Did you inform your manager that you would be late?'

'I don't have a phone at home, madam.'

'Why didn't you inform him yesterday?'

'Madam, I did not know yesterday. My daughter fell ill this morning.'

She looked at the register. 'Has your daughter been ill fourteen days of the month?'

Mahesh smirked.

'Oh, madam,' said Sharma, 'that was my other daughter. You know this virus, madam. All my daughters have been falling ill, one after the other. I have three.'

'Fourteen days,' she repeated, shaking her head.

'Yes madam, three daughters with this virus. Well, madam, I should be getting along.' He sauntered out of the room.

In the corridor he bumped into Gupta smoking a cigarette. 'What Gupta,' he said, 'you left me alone to face her.'

'What to do?' said Gupta. 'She has already told me off twice. She thinks it is still Indiraji's raj. Cigarette?'

'Might as well,' said Sharma, and took one. 'So, how are things with you?'

Gupta lit his cigarette. 'All right, so so.' He gave a bashful smile. 'My parents are searching for a girl for me. I have to get married before December. The astrologer has said that the two years after December will be very inauspicious for marriage.'

'Are you looking for a working girl, or what?'

'Yes. We think that might be preferable. How can we manage on my salary? But they bring less dowry. And my sister has to be married off next month. It is very difficult.'

'So, anything fixed up yet?'

'No, I have seen four girls so far. All dark.'

'Do not worry, Gupta. You will surely find a fair bride. Now, how about some chai?'

'Good idea.'

They strolled to the canteen and ordered tea. It arrived, steaming hot, and they drank it with satisfaction. 'Terrible tea,' said Sharma. 'This company has no care for its employees. They are stingy even in the tea they give us – no milk, no sugar. This tea is worth ten paisa. They charge us fifty paisa. Then they say it is subsidised. Ha! Subsidised!'

'Why should they care?' said Gupta. 'They only want to make money. Profit, profit, profit. That is all they care about. We are the ones who do all the work and they are the ones who benefit. This is life.'

Sharma sighed. 'Yes, this is life,' he echoed. 'Give me another cigarette, Gupta. After tea a cigarette is a must.'

They both had another.

'How is your Mrs?' asked Gupta.

Sharma grinned self-consciously. 'She is going to become a mother.'

'Arre!' exclaimed Gupta. 'What are you doing, Sharmaji? You already have three and the Government says one or two, bas.'

'They are all girls, Gupta. Who will look after us in our old age?'

'Forgive me, Sharmaji,' Gupta said, clicking his tongue, 'but I am talking to you as old friend. You already have three daughters. You will have to spend all your money marrying them off. And now one more is coming. Suppose that too is a girl?'

Sharma sighed heavily. 'That is in God's hands. After all, it is fate. I have to suffer in this life for the sins I have committed in my previous life.' He sighed again. 'Gupta, yar, it is so difficult to manage these days. Since my daughters were born I have been putting aside fifty rupees every month for their marriages. Even then it will not be enough to marry them off.'

Gupta patted Sharma. 'Why worry about the future? Deal with things as they come. Think yourself fortunate that at least you are in the purchase department.'

'That is true, that is true,' agreed Sharma. 'Where would a mere clerk's salary take me?'

They ordered some more tea and smoked another cigarette. For some time there was an amiable silence. Then Gupta leaned towards Sharma confidentially. 'Have you heard the latest?'

'What?'

'You don't know?'

'No what?'

'You won't believe it.'

'Arre, tell me Gupta.'

'Miss Das smokes.'

'Impossible!'

'Yes, yes, she smokes. Rahul saw her smoking.'

'Where?'

'In a restaurant in Connaught Place.'

'Alone?'

'No, not alone. She was sitting with a man and smoking. And when she saw Rahul, she stubbed it out.'

'I cannot believe it.'

'Even I find it difficult to believe.'

'She has a boyfriend?'

'Must be having a boyfriend.'

'Is she engaged?'

'Don't know. She's a quiet one.'

Sharma considered the news. 'Rahul is a great gossip. He talks too much. One never knows how much truth there is in what he says. He does no work, have you noticed? All he does is gossip.'

'Then you think it is not true?'

'I did not say that. It could be true. It could be untrue. Myself, I feel it is not true. Miss Das does not look the smoking kind. She appears to be a good girl.'

'But why should Rahul make it up? What does he have against her?'

'Yes, yes, you have a point. Truly, this is disturbing. But she must be engaged. She does not seem to be the kind to go around with men.'

'Maybe. Maybe not.'

Sharma chewed his lips. He shook his head. 'I will find out.'

Gupta looked at his watch. He got up. 'Sharmaji, it is already 11.30. We had better go to our departments.'

Sharma pulled him down. 'Stop acting so conscientious. No one will miss us. Lunchtime is at 12.30. We might as well stay here till lunch is over.'

Gupta looked worried. 'I am not conscientious,' he disclaimed. 'It is just that my boss has been after my life these days. If he knows I'm here he'll again say that I don't work.'

'Oh, *sit* down,' said Sharma. 'Even my boss is after my life. They are all like that, these managers. They think that only they work. Just because they stay here after office hours they expect people to believe that they work. Ha! All that is to impress the general manager. How else can they get their promotions? All maska.'

Gupta sat down.

'Jagdish,' called Sharma, 'More chai.'

The third round of tea arrived.

The electricity went off.

'Bas,' said Sharma, 'Now who can work? These power cuts will kill us all.' He sat back in his chair.

'My boss says that it is no excuse,' said Gupta gloomily. 'He says that if a power cut lasts three hours it doesn't mean that we don't work for three hours. He says that we are here to work.'

'He can keep saying that,' said Sharma contemptuously. 'Does

32

he think we're animals? They all think that we have no feelings. Work all day, work when the electricity goes off, work without increments, work without promotions, work, work, work. That is all they care about. No concern for us as human beings.'

'Hai Ram,' Gupta whispered. 'Don't look behind you. She's here.'

'Who?'

'Miss Das. She's seen us.'

'So what if she's seen us?'

'She'll tell our managers.'

'Let her tell them.'

'Sharmaji, I have already been warned.'

'Nothing to worry about. What can he do to you? The union will support you.'

'Sharmaji, it will be in my records if they give me a warning letter.'

'So let it be in your records, Gupta. Anyway you are in their bad books.'

'Suppose they give me a charge-sheet?'

'Now you are panicking. Relax. Nothing can happen. Now we have a union.'

'She's gone. Sharmaji, I'm going back to the department.'

'Arre, Gupta, sit down. Just half an hour for the lunch break. We will both go back to our departments after lunch.'

'No, no, I am going now. Excuse me, Sharmaji, see you later.' He rushed out.

Sharma shook his head. Everyone was scared. That was the problem. He opened the newspaper lying on the table and read for some time. The same news. Nothing changed. He yawned.

'There you are, Sharmaji.' It was Harish, the peon from the purchase department. 'Borwankar Sahib is calling you to his office.' He chuckled. 'He is in a bad temper. There will be fireworks today!'

Sharma looked at him unsmilingly. 'It is lunchtime. Tell him I will come after lunch.'

'Sharmaji, you had better go now. He is in a very bad temper.'

'You don't tell me what to do. You have given me the message. Now go.'

Harish smacked his forehead in despair. 'All right, all right, I will go. Don't tell me later that I did not warn you.' He left.

Sharma curled his lips contemptuously. He leaned further against his chair. He scratched an unshaven cheek. From his pocket he took out a paan wrapped in a piece of paper and put it in his mouth. Contemplatively, he chewed.

'Should we eat, Sharmaji?' It was Gupta.

'Back so soon?' asked Sharma, surprised.

'Yes, it is 12.30 – lunchtime,' Gupta said happily.

'I haven't got my lunch,' said Sharma sadly. 'Last week my wife left for her mother's with the girls for a month. I have no time to cook.'

'Why didn't you tell me earlier, Sharmaji?' exclaimed Gupta. 'You mustn't keep such problems from old friends. From tomorrow, till your wife comes home, I will ask my mother to pack extra lunch. It will be enough for both of us.'

'Gupta,' said Sharma emotionally, 'you are a true friend.'

'It is nothing.'

They shared Gupta's lunch. Then they went down to the dhaba opposite the building. There they ordered puri-aloo. It was a wonderful meal. Then they each had a large glass of lassi. After it was over they sat back, replete, content, drowsy.

'Gupta,' said Sharma, rubbing his stomach, 'I am falling asleep.'

'Me too,' groaned Gupta. 'I cannot keep my eyes open. Hai Ram.'

The heat, their meal and the lassi were having their effect. They could barely keep awake. Sleep . . . wonderful sleep.

'They should have a rest room in the office where we could take a short nap after lunch,' said Gupta. 'Then we would be ready to work, refreshed.'

'Yes,' sighed Sharma. 'In the summer especially, one cannot keep awake after lunch.'

'Sharmaji, it is already half an hour past lunchtime. Let us go back.'

Reluctantly, Sharma rose. He blinked his eyes against the afternoon sun. This was torture. Slowly, they began walking back to the building.

Suddenly Sharma stopped. 'Paan,' he said. 'I must have a paan. Let us go to the paan shop.'

Gupta hesitated. 'All right,' he said, 'but let us hurry.'

At the paan shop they bought four paans, ate one each and had the other two wrapped up. When they reached the office building they found that the electricity had not returned. They could not take the lift.

'I will die,' said Sharma. 'I cannot climb up four floors after a meal like that.' He sat down on the steps.

Mohan passed him on the way upstairs. He hooted with laughter. 'Sharmaji, everyone does it, why can't you? Kaamchor!' He bounded up the stairs before Sharma could respond.

'Haramzada,' muttered Sharma. 'Even the peons in the personnel department are getting too big for their boots.' He got up and slowly began climbing up the stairs with Gupta. 'And they expect us to work in these conditions,' he said. 'They think we are animals.'

Gupta clicked his tongue in sympathy.

On the third floor Sharma said, 'If I don't have some tea I will collapse.'

'In this heat, Sharmaji?'

'I am tired, I am sleepy. Only tea will do the job. Chalo, let us go to the canteen.'

'Sharmaji, you go. My boss has been taking rounds of our office '

'Sharma, could you please come to my office?' It was Mr Borwankar, Sharma's boss.

Gupta slid away to his department.

Sharma sighed. 'Yes, Borwankar Sahib. I will come.'

He followed his manager to his office.

'Sit down.'

Sharma sighed and sat.

'I had called you to my office more than an hour ago.'

'It was lunchtime, sir.'

'Indeed.'

'Yes, sir.'

'What happened after lunch?'

'I am here sir, after lunch.'

'It is forty-five minutes past lunchtime.'

'I went to the dhaba to eat, sir. There was a long queue there, so I was delayed, sir. All this was because my daughters have been

35

getting the virus, sir, and my wife has no time to pack lunch for me, sir. I am sure you understand, sir. After all, how can I work on an empty stomach? I feel so weak these days sir, so tired. I think I am also getting the virus.'

'Where have you been all morning?'

'Here, sir.'

'Here – where?'

'In the department, sir.'

'You were not at your desk all morning.'

'Sir, what are you saying? I must have gone down to the personnel department or the accounts department for some work.'

'What work?'

Sharma was silent. He shook his head. He looked sadly at Mr Borwankar. He said, 'Borwankar sahib, why are you taking this tone with me? You ask me questions as though you have no faith in me. This is not a detective agency. Why must you interrogate me in this manner? All right, I was not in my department, but that was because I had work in other departments. Still, if it is your wish, I will not go to other departments even if I have work there. I will sit at my desk and work only at my desk. Yes, yes, I will do that. The company does not want me to consult other departments. All right, I will not consult other departments. You will see, work will suffer, but why should I care when you do not? I have been in this company for twenty-five years, but no one cares. For twenty-five years the company has bled me, sucked me dry. What do you know? You have been here only two years. You know nothing. Twenty-five years ago I joined as a clerk. Today I am still a clerk. Why should I work?'

His outburst had touched something raw in him. Overwhelmed and defiant, he glared at Mr Borwankar.

'Sharma, you still haven't answered my question.'

Sharma shrugged his shoulders. 'Borwankar sahib, what is the point of answering? Even if I answer, you will not believe me.' He reflected and said sadly, 'No, there is no point telling you anything. What can you understand?'

Mr Borwankar said dryly, 'I understand that you haven't been at your desk all morning. You were seen loitering in the corridor and drinking tea in the canteen. Presumably that is what you did all morning. And that is what you have been doing virtually every day. In addition, you never come to work on time. Today you were half-an-hour late. This is your fourteenth late arrival this month. Last month you were late twenty days and the previous month, fifteen days. What do you have to say for yourself?'

'What can I say? This is the only work the personnel department has. Every day they sit and count how many late arrivals there are. For that they get paid. Even I can count.'

'Sharma, you are evading all my questions. I have already warned you three times. Each time you gave me to understand that things would change. Nothing has changed. Your work output is zero. Your attitude leaves much to be desired.'

There was a knock at the door and the personnel officer entered. She sat next to Sharma. Mr Borwankar said, 'Under the circumstances I have no alternative but to give you this.' He gave Sharma a typed sheet of paper.

Sharma read it slowly. It was a charge-sheet accusing him of being absent from his workplace all morning and of coming late to work on specified days. If he did not answer in twenty-four hours it would be presumed that he had accepted the charges.

His hands trembled. So. After twenty-five years – this.

He tossed the paper back to Mr Borwankar and got up. He said, 'You can keep your piece of paper.'

'Sharmaji,' said Miss Das, 'please accept it. Not accepting a charge-sheet is a very serious offence.'

Sharma replied, 'I will do nothing without consulting the general secretary of the workers' union.'

He walked out of the room.

Sharma found Adesh Singh, general secretary of the workers' union on the production floor, listlessly assembling some components. He walked up to him and said, 'I want to talk to you, come to the canteen.'

Adesh's supervisor looked up from the end of the table. Adesh went up to her. 'Madam,' he said, 'please excuse me for ten minutes. Something serious has come up.'

She replied, 'Adesh, you know I cannot permit time for union activities during office hours. Go in the tea break.'

Adesh continued standing before her. After some time he said, 'Madam, may I go to the canteen to drink some water?'

'You are not thirsty.'

He looked at her in amazement. He said, 'Who are you to say that I am not thirsty? Madam, you surprise me. You permit everyone to go to the bathroom or to the canteen for a drink of water. In fact, they do not even ask your permission to go. Why do you make an exception in my case? Is it because I am the general secretary of the union? Does the general secretary have no right to be thirsty? Have things come to such a pass that a worker is denied *water*? Is this the management's new rule?'

'Go, please go.'

'Yes, madam, I will go. I do not need permission from you to quench my thirst. There has been no electricity most of this morning. And yet you deny me water.'

The other workers listened, rapt.

With his hand on his chest, Adesh said, 'Madam, what you have said has hurt me here . . . right here.' He drew a shuddering breath. 'You think we have no feelings, no hearts. You think that only officers have feelings. But madam, believe me, our hearts are more vulnerable than yours. We feel . . . we feel. Sharmaji, chalo.'

With dignity, he walked out of the production floor, Sharma trailing behind him. In the canteen, Adesh wiped his brow. 'Yes, Sharmaji. Now what has happened?'

'What can I tell you? They have given me a charge-sheet.'

'What does it say?'

'That I haven't been in my office all morning and that I don't come to work on time.'

'Is that true?'

'What does that matter? What truth is there in this world?'

Adesh picked his teeth reflectively. 'So, what do you want me to do?'

'You tell me.'

'Accept the charge-sheet. Deny the charges. What else?'

'Then they'll institute an enquiry.'

'Let them. They need witnesses for that. No worker will be a witness.'

'The officers will. Mr Borwankar will. Miss Das will. And those latecomings are on record.'

'Then accept the charges. They'll let you off with a warning letter.'

'How can you say that?'

'I'll see to that.'

'All right. But you come with me to Borwankar sahib.'

They both meditated for some time.

'Some chai?' asked Adesh.

'Yes, of course.'

They ordered tea. Sharma lit a cigarette and smoked sadly.

'Sharmaji,' said Adesh deliberately, 'you had better mend your ways. I can't help you out next time.'

The tea arrived.

'What do you mean, mend my ways?' asked Sharma sulkily.

'You know what I mean. You don't seem to know your limits.'

'Don't lecture me. You are the general secretary of the union. Your duty is to get me out of this, not give me speeches.'

'You keep quiet. If you want me to help you, hold your tongue.'

Sharma simmered. Again, insults from someone so much younger. They finished their tea. 'Chalo,' said Adesh. They went to Mr Borwankar's office and knocked on the door.

'Come in.' They entered. He was talking to the personnel officer. 'Please sit down.' They sat.

'Please show me the charge-sheet,' said Adesh.

'Why are you here, Adesh?' asked Mr Borwankar.

'Why not? You have the personnel officer as your witness. Sharmaji has me as his. Who knows what false accusations the management is making against the poor man.'

Mr Borwankar handed the charge-sheet to Sharma. Adesh took it from Sharma and read it. He looked up, shock registering on his face. 'What is all this, Borwankar sahib? Madam, what does this mean?'

'Isn't that evident?' replied Mr Borwankar.

'No, it isn't. Sharmaji was at his desk all morning. I saw him there.'

'And what, pray, were you doing in the purchase department all morning?'

'Borwankar sahib, you cannot intimidate me. I do not work under you. If anyone can question me, it is my supervisor. She had sent me there on some work. I had to check up on some material. You are not the only person who has work outside your room. We all do. There are other workers who saw Sharmaji at his desk.'

You will get proof. I can get any number of workers to give it in writing that Sharmaji was at his desk all morning.'

'Indeed. Go ahead. All that can be investigated when there is an enquiry. Sharma, will you please sign the copy and accept the charge-sheet? Enough time has been wasted.'

Sharma and Adesh exchanged glances.

'Sign it,' said Adesh.

Sharma took the letter and signed the copy. He got up. He said, 'Madam, advise the company to change its attitude to workers. Giving charge-sheets left and right is not the answer.' He left.

Adesh looked accusingly at Mr Borwankar. 'Sir,' he said. 'Do you know what you are doing to that man? You have broken him. You have betrayed him.'

'Adesh,' said Mr Borwankar wearily. 'Please spare me the dramatics.'

'Ask him to speak to me,' said Miss Das.

Adesh nodded. 'All right, I'll do that. Tell me, do you intend to hold an enquiry?'

'That depends on whether he accepts the charges, doesn't it?'

'Sir, I request you to let him off with a warning letter this time. I will talk to him. I will din some sense into his thick head. I will see to it that he changes his ways. His wife and children are away these days. He is lonely. He is unwell.'

Miss Das said, 'I thought his daughter was ill and that was why he was late today?'

'That is true. His family left this afternoon. From today he is all alone. He is lost. Madam, why are you asking questions? You as a personnel officer should understand.'

She smiled faintly. 'I do,' she said. 'Ask him to speak to me.'

Adesh said, 'So there will be no enquiry?'

There was a pause. Miss Das said, 'He must accept the charges and apologise in writing.'

Adesh shook his head. 'Yes, yes, you must have your pound of flesh. Yes, I will tell him.' He rose wearily.

Miss Das was in her office when Sharma entered.

'Come in, Sharmaji, please sit down.'

Sharma sighed and sat. He passed his hand over his brow. 'It is so hot,' he said. 'How do you expect us to work with these power cuts, Miss Das?'

'What to do, Sharmaji? That is how life is in Delhi. Would you like a glass of cold water?'

'Certainly.' He gulped down the water. 'What advantages there are to being an officer! You have flasks of cold water in your room. We poor workers have to go to the canteen to drink water. And when we go there and someone sees that we are not at our workplace, we are accused of shirking work.' He returned the glass. 'Thank you, madam.'

'You're welcome.'

There was a short silence and then she said, 'Sharmaji, it seems that you are greatly distressed. What is the matter?'

Sharma gave a short laugh. 'What a question to ask! You give me a charge-sheet and then you ask me why I am distressed. What madam, does the personnel department not know even this much?'

'I'm sorry, that's not what I meant. I meant that you have been looking run down and depressed for the last few days.'

Sharma looked at her in wonder. 'So,' he said, '*someone* has noticed. Yes, madam, I have been run down and depressed the last few days. I have been run down and depressed the last few months, the last several years. I do not remember what happiness is, madam . . . I cannot remember. And if I do remember, it is so distant a fragment of the past that I feel . . . maybe it never was. The future stretches before me like the night. Ah, madam, what can I tell you? What do you know of life? You are still young, you are not even married. Make the most of this time, madam, it will never return. With marriage, children and careers – much is lost madam, much is lost. You know nothing yet, nothing. When you were sitting there with Borwankar sahib, I thought, poor Miss Das, already she is so involved in office politics. Soon even she will be corrupted. She sees that I, an employee twenty-five years in the company is given a charge-sheet. I, who have given my best years to the company. She sees. Does she feel anything? Does she care? If she feels, she cannot show it. But maybe she does feel. Maybe her heart goes out to this man. She has to do her duty. She has to be there. But maybe she asks herself, what is happening? Should this be happening? And maybe, something deep within her answers, no it should not. Maybe her heart beats in silent sympathy

41

for this man so completely broken by the company's cruel policies. But she can say nothing. She is after all, in the personnel department. And the personnel department has to be diplomatic. It sees and hears all, it can say nothing. I understand. I do not blame you. But madam, beware. You know nothing of the evils surrounding you. You are too innocent. You do not know what people say, the rumours they spread. Look at me. You must have heard how people talk about me. They make me out to be sometimes a rakshash, sometimes a Harijan. They say I am a bad influence on people. They say I do not work. They say people should not mix with me. I, who was one of the first people to join the company twenty-five years ago. If I did not work, why did the company give me a special award for excellent work twenty years ago? You look surprised. You do not know. Of course, they will not tell you. They know you are intelligent. They know you will ask, what has happened to this man? You wish to know madam, yes?

'Madam, what can I tell you? Where can I begin? What was I then? What am I now! That Mahesh in your department, I was his age when I joined this company. Look at him. He is too big for his boots. He tells me I'm late. He flaunts his power just because he is in the personnel department. Madam, keep an eye on him. He is dangerous. He will alienate everyone from the personnel department if he continues this way. Let me tell you something. He does no work. He sits with his register and pretends he is filling it in. Actually he is doing nothing of the sort. He is planning wicked schemes. He is counting how many times Gupta and I are late. Madam, do you know how often other people are late? No you do not. That is because Mahesh does not give you their names. He gives names of only some people. I happen to be one of those unfortunate few. Madam, keep an eye on him. He is crooked. He will only give you the information that suits him. He will let you down, madam. You are too trusting. That is good. That is also bad. People will take advantage of you. Like they took advantage of me. Once, many years ago, even I was like you; trusting and innocent. I believed everything I was told. I worked hard. Not once was I late. And people said, look at Sharma, he is our best worker. I got an award. And after that – nothing. Other people rose. Other people got increments. Other people got promotions. Poor Sharma got left behind. Other people buttered their bosses.

And I, fool that I was, I believed that only hard work succeeds. Did Srivastava become purchase officer through hard work? Was Tiwari promoted from peon to clerk because he worked hard? No, they all did maska. They accompanied their managers to their homes. They ran personal errands for them. They did jobs for their bosses' wives. Hah! I know how they got their promotions. I refused. I was idealistic. I had principles. And here I am, still a clerk. Now *those* men order me around, tell me, Sharma do this, Sharma do that. And Sharma does it, even though inside, his heart is breaking. Madam, some more water, if I may.'

She gave him another glass of water. She said, 'Sharmaji, I did not know all this.'

He drank the water and wiped his mouth. 'Madam, you know nothing. Even now, you know nothing. You don't know what goes on in this place.'

'What?'

He looked behind him at the door. He got up and opened it. No one. He sat at his chair and leaned forward. In hushed tones, he said, 'Dhanda of girls.'

'I don't understand.'

'Madam, forgive me, you are too innocent. I will keep quiet. I should not have mentioned it.' He looked behind him again. He paused. He whispered. 'When girls are recruited in this company, they have to perform certain favours for certain men for having got in.'

'Oh.'

'I have shocked you, madam. Forgive me. But it is true.' He leaned closer to the desk. He said, 'These men are still working here. These girls are still working here. So much dirt, madam. What can you understand of these things?'

'Who are these men?'

He leaned back. 'I cannot reveal their names, madam.'

'Why not? You can help me remove this dirt.'

'Oh no, madam, no, no.'

'Why not, Sharmaji?'

'No, madam, no. Do not ask me why.'

'But if you don't tell me, Sharmaji, it will continue.'

Sharma smiled gently. 'But you see, it is not happening now. It is a thing of the past. Since you joined the company such things have stopped. People are scared. They say that a woman has come to the personnel department and that this woman is honest. She will protect our girls. Now there is nothing to worry about. Rest assured, madam. All is well, now that you are here.'

'All is not well, Sharmaji. How can all be well when you continue coming late to work every other day and are never at your workplace?'

'Madam, madam, madam.' Sharma wagged an admonishing finger at her. 'You are very persistent. That is your job. You are personnel officer. That is your duty. Good. That is good.'

'So, Sharmaji, what happened today?'

'What can I say, madam? Sometimes I curse fate for bringing me into this world, for flinging me amid such people. Often I ask myself – what sins did I commit in my last birth to suffer so in this one? There is no answer. God has his own ways, madam, who knows why, who knows how?

'I see you are smiling madam. I know what you are thinking. You are thinking – this Sharma talks too much. Why is Sharma saying all this? Sharma has not answered my question. But I have, madam, I have. Reflect carefully over all that I have told you. You will find the answers. There are no simple answers to simple questions. I read a poem once, an English poem that was translated into Hindi. Somewhere it said:

> "There are no small questions for small men
> All men are Hamlet on an empty street
> Or a windy quay
> All men are Lear in the market
> When the tradesmen have gone."

'Madam, if he had not written the poem, I would have written it. Even here someone has done it before me. Can you understand what he is saying, madam? You nod your head. Then you understand me. Your questions are answered, madam. Madam, some more water, please.'

She poured out another glass of water. He drank it thirstily. 'Sharmaji, may I make a request?'

'Madam, any request.'

'From tomorrow you will make an effort to come to work on time?'

'Of course, madam, of course.'

'And I don't want to see you in the canteen or corridors during office hours.'

'Whatever you say, madam, whatever you say.'

'Thank you.'

Sharma gazed at her fondly. 'Do not thank me, madam. Why are you thanking me?' He paused. He said, 'Madam, you have made a request. I agreed. Now may I make one?'

'Certainly.'

'Put in a word for me to Borwankar sahib, madam. In his mind it is set that Sharma is bad. Once such an impression is made, it does not change. In this company especially. Tell Borwankar sahib, Sharma once got a special award. Tell him, his promotion is long overdue. Tell him, is it fair that Sharma remains a clerk for twenty-five years? You have influence, madam. You are personnel officer. If you tell Borwankar sahib, Borwankar sahib will listen.'

'Sharmaji, now everything depends on you. I can do nothing.'

Sharma sighed. 'Yes, that is what they all say. Well, you have been kind, madam. You have patiently listened to me. Madam, do you like cosmetics . . . lipsticks?'

'Like what, Sharmaji?'

'I can get these things very cheap, madam, even free. After all I am in the purchase department. I can get you imported scents and lipsticks, electronic items, cassettes.'

'How?'

'Oh, come, come, madam. What can I get you?'

'Nothing, thank you, Sharmaji.'

Sharma nodded his head seriously. 'You are absolutely right in refusing. Even I refuse. They keep telling me, Sharmaji, please take this, Sharmaji, please take that. They say, you place such large orders for your company; let us give you some gifts to show you our appreciation. But I say, no. No. I am not like the rest. I will not give to anyone, I will not take from anyone. For that they respect me. After all, if there is no self-respect, then what is there?

'Well, madam, I must leave. Here is my answer to the charge-sheet.' He handed the paper to Miss Das.

She read it. She said, 'So, you have denied being absent from the workplace, saying that your manager is victimising you. You have accepted coming late to work, saying that your children have been ill. And you have apologised if this has caused any misunderstanding. Sharmaji!'

'Madam, madam, let us not argue any more. You asked me to apologise. I have apologised. Now let bygones be bygones. Let a new chapter begin.'

Miss Das put the paper away. 'Some more water, Sharmaji?'

'No, madam, thank you.' He rose from his chair. 'I must be leaving.'

'Don't hesitate to come to me if you have any problems.'

'Madam, I do not have any problems. Borwankar sahib has problems. Mahesh has problems. Even your peon Mohan has problems. Yes, if they continue to have problems, I will come to you.'

He got up and was about to leave the room when a thought seemed to strike him. He appeared to hesitate, and then spoke. 'Madam, before I leave, I must ask you a question of a rather personal nature. As a brother, I would like to ask you. Please do not mind.'

'Yes?'

'Madam, you have a good job, you are young. Like an elder brother, let me give you some advice. You must not postpone marriage, no woman should be alone in this world. I am speaking out of concern for you. Maybe, you are already engaged?'

'I am married.'

Sharma reeled. 'Madam!'

She began to laugh.

'But madam, you are *Miss* Das.'

'Yes, I've retained my maiden name.'

'Why?'

'Why not?'

Sharma considered. 'A woman goes into another family. She must take the name of the family.'

'I have not gone into any family. My husband and I are both working.'

Sharma stared at her. 'You are very modern.'

'And that is bad?'

He reflected. 'Maybe not. I cannot say. When did this take place, madam?'

'Two months ago.'

'Madam, forgive me for saying this, but this is very bad, very very bad. You did not tell any of us. You did not distribute any sweets. I am greatly offended. This is a cause for celebration, not secrecy.'

'It was no secret, Sharmaji.'

'Oh well.' He surveyed her. 'You don't even look married. No sindoor, no mangalsutra, no jewellery. What is this, madam?'

'No need for all that, Sharmaji.'

Sharma shook his head in despair. 'What can I say? I suppose things are changing. I would like to meet your husband, madam. Is he also good and kind like you?'

She looked confused. 'You will certainly meet him one day.'

'Good. Very good. Well, madam, I will go. From my side, please say namaste to your husband.'

'Certainly.'

With great dignity he sailed out of the room. A minute later he returned. 'Madam,' he said with a slight shrug, 'I was wondering, you wouldn't be interested in reading some of my poetry would you?'

'I would very much like to.'

Sharma smiled. He nodded. 'I will get them tomorrow. Madam, I wrote these poems many, many years ago. Since then I have written nothing, nothing at all. Still . . . they are very philosophical, very deep, very complex. Tomorrow, at 9 am I will share them with you.'

She replied, 'In the lunch break.'

He frowned. 'There will be another power cut in the afternoon. How can I read my poetry to you, drenched in sweat?' He considered.

She smiled.

He capitulated. 'If you insist, then, the lunch break.'

Outside the office, Sharma looked at his watch. It was already 5 pm, just half an hour left for office to get over. Slowly he walked down the corridor, softly humming an old love song to himself. Suddenly he was flooded with memories. Once . . . years ago, he had loved, loved madly, crazily. Her large kajal-filled eyes had haunted him, bewitched him. Those eyes . . . those eyes. He would have gladly died for her. Shy, smitten, he had said nothing.

47

She had never known. Sharma stopped and swallowed. He felt his heart would burst. Twenty-five years.

'Sharmaji, coming to the canteen?' It was Gupta, bounding down the stairs, two at a time.

Sharma smiled indulgently. 'Not scared of your boss now?'

'He has gone out of the office on some work. Chalo, let us have some chai, Sharmaji.'

Gently, Sharma shook his head. 'I have some work.' He patted Gupta. 'You go.'

Gupta stared at him, open-mouthed.

'Gupta,' said Sharma, 'Miss Das does not have a boyfriend. She is married. People in this office are always spreading dirty rumours. Do not listen to them.'

He gave Gupta a final pat and walked to his department, still humming. When he entered the room his fellow clerks grinned.

'You are an elusive man, Sharmaji,' said Rahul. 'Everyone has been looking for you today. Where were you?'

Sharma shrugged his shoulders modestly. 'There were things to do, many things to do. And there is still so much to be done. Rahul, life is very brief, very fleeting.'

Rahul chuckled. 'All right, Sharmaji, I will leave you to your considerations.' He went back to his typing.

Sharma sat on his desk. He took the paan out of his pocket and carefully removed its wrapping. He put it in his mouth. Chewing, he opened his drawer and took out a sheet of paper. Lovingly, he placed it on his desk, licked his pencil and began a new poem.

The Prophecy

◆

In the end we decided to visit the astrologer before going to the gynaecologist. After an hour's wait in the relentless afternoon sun, a scooter finally stopped for us. When we told the scooterwalla where we wanted to go, he snorted and spat out a copious stream of paan.

'I don't go such short distances,' he said contemptuously. We turned away wearily. 'It will be ten rupees!' he shouted.

'Go to hell,' said Amrita. 'You scooterwallas are all the same.'

I dragged her back. 'Forget your principles today. We'll both collapse in this heat.'

We sat inside the scooter. To the scooterwalla's left was a picture of Goddess Lakshmi with a tinsel garland around it, to his right, one of a film actress, bare-bosomed and smiling. Surveying us through the rear view mirror, the scooterwalla grinned. He lit a beedi with a flourish and started the scooter. Loudly and at breakneck speed, the scooter weaved its way through the traffic. We clung to the sides and helplessly tried to hold our sarees down.

'Maybe I'll be lucky and have a miscarriage now,' gasped Amrita.

'Slow down,' I shouted above the noise of the scooter. He accelerated. 'Slow down will you!'

He turned to me, grinning. 'What did you say?'

I screamed, 'Look at the road, don't look at me! Slow down!'

He missed a car by an inch, swerved violently, threw back his head and laughed. 'Which college are you from?' We did not answer. He accelerated.

'Slow down! Do you want us to die!'

'Memsahib,' he said, 'death is neither in your hands or in mine. If we have to die, we will die. It is all written down.'

'You die if you want to. At the rate you're going you'll kill us too.'

He bounded up and down in his seat gleefully. 'Who cares,' he sang, 'Who cares if I die, who cares if you die, what difference does it make!'

'Stop talking to him,' Amrita told me, 'he's enjoying it.'

The scooterwalla accelerated again and looked at me hopefully in the rear view mirror. I looked out at the road. We had passed our destination. '*Stop, stop!*'

He turned to me again and winked. 'What is there to be so scared about? People die all the time.'

'*Will you please stop, we've passed the place!*'

He braked immediately and we almost fell over him. He leered at our bosoms and said, 'Madam, you should have warned me. This is how accidents happen.'

I thrust a ten rupee note into his outstretched hand. He took it, caressing my hands as he did, smiled slowly and drove off. Shakily we began walking to Chachaji's house. Chachaji, as the astrologer was called, was very popular with the girls in our college. His prophecies came true and he was cheaper than the rest. He could read your minds. One look at you and he knew everything – your past, your present, your future.

His wife opened the door to us and led us to the living room. I could hear the pressure cooker in the kitchen and the house was redolent with the smell of chicken curry. Somewhere inside a baby cried. The smell of incense wafted in and Chachaji entered. Spotless white pyjama-kurta, soft white beard, frail frame, startling eyes . . . mystic . . . ethereal. We stared at him, dumbstruck.

He sat opposite us and gazed into our faces. He smiled. 'Yes, my children?'

I looked at Amrita. It had been her idea to come here. When she didn't say anything, I spoke. 'We wanted to consult you.'

'Yes, yes, they all want to consult me.' How soft his voice was.

I looked again at Amrita. Her eyes were deep with tears. I knew how she felt. I could have confessed anything to him.

He turned to Amrita. Almost imperceptibly, he shook his head. 'Beti, you are in a forest, lost, wandering. You do not know where

to go.' Dumbly, Amrita nodded. He sighed and closed his eyes. 'I
see a boy.' We started. 'I see trouble. It all began with this boy.
What is the date, time and place of your birth?' She told him. On
a piece of paper he did some rapid calculations. He shook his head.
'The stars are not good. The shadow of Shani is falling on you. It
is a very unlucky year for you.'

Amrita whispered. 'Chachaji, what will happen?'

'Happen? Has it not already happened?'

She flinched and lowered her eyes. Her fingers gathered and
ungathered her pleats. 'What will I do, Chachaji, what will I do?'

He closed his eyes once again. I was sweating profusely and
there were beads of perspiration above Amrita's mouth.

His wife entered with two glasses of water for us. We drank
thirstily. She smiled at us. 'You are both so pretty.' We smiled
gratefully. 'But you don't know how to wear sarees,' she said,
clicking her tongue. 'Stand up for a moment.' We stood up
obediently. She bent and pulled our sarees down. 'Always wear
your sandals before wearing sarees. Or else it'll ride high,' she
adjusted our pleats, then stood up and surveyed her work with
satisfaction.

'Champa's mother,' sighed Chachaji, 'they have not come here
to talk of sarees.'

'Oh you,' she dismissed him with a gesture. 'Don't frighten
these children with all your talk.' She picked up the glasses, gave
us another sunny smile and walked out of the room, her payals
tinkling softly.

Apologetically, we looked at Chachaji. He smiled indulgently.
'Yes, children, what else do you want to know?'

'What should I do?' asked Amrita.

'I will do a puja for you. It will negate the bad influence of
Shani. After six months I will perform a second puja. Your stars
will change. The shadow of Shani will no longer envelop you.'
Worshipfully, we nodded. 'For the puja,' he continued, his eyes
fixed at the wall behind us, 'you will have to give a donation.'

'How much?' Amrita asked, fumbling in her purse.

'Whatever you wish, beti, whatever you wish. With the blessings of God all will be well. I will do a special puja for you.'

Amrita gave him twenty rupees. He took it and fingered the
notes meditatively. 'My child, this will suffice only for a small

51

puja. For you I will have to perform a big puja. Or else the trouble may become worse.'

'Chachaji, I have very little money.'

He shrugged his shoulders. 'If that is your wish, then. This may not suffice to negate the evil influence of Shani.' I took out ten rupees from my bag and gave it to him. 'Chachaji, this is all we have.'

He smiled, took the money with one hand, and patted my cheek with the other. 'You are a true friend, beti. You are a loyal friend. Your stars are good. You will do an MA. It is possible that you will work. You will marry a handsome man and have one son, one daughter.'

'When will I get married, Chachaji?'

'How old are you?'

'Seventeen.'

'In six, seven years, beti.'

'Will it be arranged?'

'It will be love. You will have a love marriage.'

'Will I go abroad, Chachaji?'

'Many times, many, many times.'

'Thank you, Chachaji,' I said, quietly ecstatic.

He turned to Amrita. 'After I perform the puja, your stars will change. You will marry a handsome, fair, rich, influential man. You will have two sons who will rise to powerful positions in the government. They will bring you power, fame, respect. And you will also travel abroad, many, many times.'

He rose. We folded our hands.

The heat hit us as we stepped out of the house. We walked towards the bus stop.

'Oh no, Patram!' I gasped and pulled Amrita back from the road. In silence, breathing heavily, we stood where we were. A khaki-clad man walked past us. He was not Patram. Feeling foolish, we continued walking.

Patram was the omnipresent, omniscient peon-cum-bodyguard-cum-regulator-of-rules, employed by our college, who watched the boarders like a hawk and reported all our goings-on to the superintendent. He knew who sneaked out of the gates before the rules permitted, who returned after 8 pm, who smoked, who had a boyfriend. Just last month two girls had been expelled from the hostel after Patram smelt cigarette smoke in the corridor outside their room and informed the superintendent. The case went up to the principal. The girls pleaded with her but she would not budge. She said that she would not have girls of such loose character in her college. They had to leave. If someone decided to sneak out of the college gates and see a 1.30 film show, Patram was sure to know. He was everywhere – in the markets, cinema, theatres, Connaught Place. We lived in dread of the famous khaki dress and cap and the permanent grin on his face. That morning we had walked out of the college before official going-out time, and there had been no sign of Patram. Dressed in sarees for the first time in an effort to look older, we had walked out of the gates, awkwardly and with trepidation. Still no Patram.

And now, weak with relief at the false alarm, we waited for the bus that would take us to the gynaecologist. It arrived almost immediately, and for once, it was not crowded. 'Forty rupees,' Amrita said as the bus began to move. 'We've spent forty rupees today.'

I said nothing. We had just a hundred between us. We had no idea how much the gynaecologist would take. The previous day, in a desperate bid to make some money, we had gone around the hostel collecting old newspapers, empty jars and bottles. We had fitted these into six polythene bags and trudged to the nearby market, trying to appear oblivious to the noise they made as we walked, praying that the polythene bags would not fall apart. In the market we had squatted before the kabadiwalla and bargained at length. He had said he would give us twenty rupees for the whole lot. We had asked for thirty. He had refused. We walked away and he had called us back. Twenty-five, he had said. So we struck the bargain. On the way back, overcome by the sight of pastries in the bakery, we had spent most of it on black forests, lemon tarts, chocolate eclairs and chicken patties. And now we had barely enough for the gynaecologist, let alone the abortion. Maybe, I thought, she isn't pregnant after all.

The clinic was plush, beautiful and smelt rich. Our hearts sank. We sat at the reception and waited Amrita's turn. There was just one other person there, in a bright pink chiffon saree. She stared at us. We thumbed unseeingly through the magazines. She continued staring.

'She's going to ask questions,' Amrita murmured.

'Lie.'

'What?'

'So,' said the woman, 'you have come to visit Dr Kumar?'

We nodded distantly and went back to our magazines.

'How old are you both?'

'Twenty,' I lied. Beneath my saree my legs began to tremble.

'Acha? You look younger.'

Amrita smiled. 'That's good.'

She continued surveying us and her face grew grim. She drew her palla over her shoulders. 'Are you married?'

'Yes,' I said.

'No,' said Amrita.

'Acha?' She turned a shocked face towards Amrita. 'Then what are you doing here?'

'Period problems,' said Amrita and went back to her magazine.

'What problems?'

'Irregular.' I said.

'Too frequent,' said Amrita.

She smiled knowingly. 'There seems to be some confusion about the problem, yes?' We did not reply. She turned her gaze on me. 'So are you the married one?'

'Yes.'

'You don't look married. How old are you?'

'Twenty.'

'So what is *your* problem?'

'I'm accompanying my friend.'

'Acha! So the married friend is accompanying the unmarried friend to the gynaecologist!' She knew, she knew. She fingered her mangalsutra. 'It seems to me that neither of you is married.' She waited. 'And if that is so, God knows what you are doing here.'

The nurse called, 'Mrs Mehta, your turn please.'

She rose, exuding a strong whiff of Intimate as she did, and walked in.

'Bitch,' said Amrita.

Ten minutes later, Mrs Mehta emerged, gave us a meaningful look and left.

We went in, sat opposite Dr Kumar and began to cry. She was wonderful. She spoke to us in low, comforting tones, gave us tissues, got us cold water and had the nurse serve us tea. Finally, red-nosed and swollen-eyed, we were quiet.

She turned to Amrita. 'You're pregnant?'

'I think so.'

'Let me check you.'

I sat in the room while she and Amrita went into the adjoining room. When they emerged, I knew it was confirmed. Amrita sat next to me. She was trembling. I put my hand on her knee.

Dr Kumar's eyes, brown and gentle, looked troubled. She reminded me of my mother. But I could not tell my mother if I were pregnant.

'How much will an abortion cost?' asked Amrita.

Dr Kumar rested her face against her hand. 'Does the boy know?'

'No. There's no need for him to know.'

'So, you don't intend marrying him?'

'No. How much will it cost?'

Dr Kumar was silent. Finally she said, 'It's a thousand rupees in this clinic.' Amrita and I looked at each other in despair. We didn't even have a hundred. Dr Kumar, her eyes full of compassion, suggested that there were government hospitals where it could be done for about a hundred rupees. She would give us the addresses. Sensing my apprehension, she assured me that they were perfectly safe. As for the abortion – people were having it all the time. She paused, then said, 'Amrita, would you like to take your parents into your confidence?' Seeing Amrita's face, she gently continued, 'Sometimes, beti, we tend to misjudge our parents. Often they're the best people to turn to at such times.'

'Last year,' Amrita whispered, 'our neighbour's daughter got pregnant. She threw herself in front of a passing train. Her parents refused to claim her body. And my father said, that is how it should be.'

'Your mother?'

'What could she say? She cried for days. And Ma can't keep anything to herself. She'll tell my father.'

Dr Kumar seemed lost in thought. After some time she sighed and said, 'Are you both in the hostel?' We nodded. 'So, your parents are not in Delhi?' We shook our heads. 'I see.' She wrote down a few addresses and gave them to us. We rose to leave. 'Wait,' she said, and proceeded to give us a fifteen-minute talk on contraception. Wide-eyed and quivering with embarrassment, I listened. I could barely look Dr Kumar in the eye as she systematically went through it all. How did people ever buy these things? How did they look chemists in the eye? How did they ever get down to it? Amrita looked tired but unembarrassed, nodding from time to time. After Dr Kumar finished, she said, 'Don't be so foolish next time.' We got up. She said, 'Amrita, you're already two months gone. Don't wait much longer.' Amrita nodded.

Dr Kumar refused to take any money.

It was five when we reached the hostel. We changed out of our sarees and looked at each other.

'Marry him, Amrita,' I said tentatively.

'Please,' Amrita replied, 'you'll never understand.'

I didn't. I didn't understand at all. I liked Rakesh; he was handsome, bright, fun to be with. He smelt wonderfully of aftershave and had given us our first motorcycle rides. He's so *nice* I had often told Amrita, so *nice*. But she said he had no aesthetic sense. She didn't *want* nice. She didn't *want* to get married after college. She didn't *want* to end up like her parents. She wanted adventure. I, half in love with Rakesh, his aftershave and his motorcycle, was sure he would provide adventure. She scoffed at the very idea.

Often I wondered why Amrita had gone into this strange, loveless relationship. Normally so communicative with me, she was unusually reticent about her affair with Rakesh. Was it just the sex? My mind recoiled at the thought. Nevertheless, I wondered. It's nothing so great, she told me once, and I tried to school my expression at this unexpected revelation. She had done it! How often? She looked the same. On our occasional outings together, I watched them covertly. They laughed, talked, ate, drank. I could see no hidden fire in Rakesh's eyes, no answering flame in Amrita's. In my own fantasies, I was beautiful but enigmatic, virginal, but willing to surrender it all to the man I married. If it happened before marriage he would not respect me. I would tame the beast in him. Did Rakesh respect Amrita? Did she drive him crazy with desire. I waited to hear more, but she said nothing. I continued feeding my fantasies of handsome men on motorcycles, smelling of aftershave, with deep voices and British accents. I would happily have settled for one after college, happily married one. He would never tire of me, nor I of him. Marriage would be that wondrous path of rapid heartbeats and unending, intimate discoveries.

Amrita spent the weekends with Rakesh in his hostel. 'This bloody college and those frustrated spinsters make me sick,' she would tell me every Sunday evening, referring to the superintendent and the principal. 'I'll be glad to get out of this hole.' Rakesh never seemed to figure in her plans for the future. She wanted to be a journalist and I had no doubt that she would succeed. Not only did she write expressively, but had strong feelings and a strange kind of courage, an indifference to what people thought of her. While I seemed to spend my life looking over my shoulder to see who was watching, starting, for fear someone was listening, always fearful that 'they' would know. Amrita, as long as I had known her, had done exactly what she wanted. Now, on Amrita's behalf, it was I who was guilty, scared of discovery, certain that retribution was imminent.

We could not use the hostel phone to fix up the appointment as it was out of order. We began walking towards the gate again since the taxi-stand outside the college had a public phone. But Nemesis in the form of Patram was just behind us. Grinning, he led us to the superintendent's office. He had seen us outside the college gates that morning, he said. The superintendent, sullen, but with a predatory gleam in her eyes, lectured us on our dishonesty, the wickedness of our actions and on our parents' inability to inculcate in us the virtues of restraint and politeness. As she took a deep breath to renew her attack, Amrita told her that she was an ignorant, power-hungry, narrow-minded, perverse woman and stormed out of the room. Weak with shock and fear, I gave the superintendent an ingratiating smile and followed Amrita.

Back in our room, Amrita raged. She damned the college and the authorities. 'One day,' she fumed, 'I'm going to expose this place for what it is. I'll write about it and publish it. No one will want to attend this wretched place.' I replied, 'It'll have exactly the opposite effect – your article will reassure every middle-class parent like your and mine.'

We were gated for two weeks. But the next week we sneaked out and waited for a scooter or bus that would take us to one of the clinics Dr Kumar had suggested. Patram's voice called us from across the road, precipitating another return. Once again he escorted us to the superintendent's office. Our gating was extended to four weeks. Two weeks passed, then three weeks. One day someone casually mentioned that her sister had had a miscarriage after eating pickles. That evening I made Amrita eat half a bottle of mango pickle. The room smelled of it for days and she was violently sick, but nothing happened. She said, 'If I starve myself maybe it'll die,' and didn't eat for three days. She almost collapsed, but nothing happened. I said, 'Eat, you'll need your strength for the abortion.' 'When,' she whispered, 'when?' As the days passed I felt Amrita's rising fear. The more fearful she was, the quieter she became. Daily I murmured reassurances while unobtrusively examining her stomach. It seemed to grow no bigger. Would an abortion at this stage kill her? I imagined Amrita's prolonged, bloody death at the clinic, with me left behind to break the news to her parents, to the superintendent, to the principal, to my parents. The horror. Would they hold me responsible? And then I was ridden with guilt for thinking such thoughts, for feeling not sorrow, but terror for the seemingly endless repercussions of such a death. My fantasies turned to nightmares.

As our gating entered the fourth week, Amrita fell ill. She refused to let me call a doctor for fear he would find out that she was pregnant. At midnight her temperature rose to 104 degrees. The superintendent did not take kindly to my knock at her door at that hour, urging her to call a doctor. This was no time to come knocking at her door, she snapped, handing me two aspirins and banging the door on my face. I stood outside her door for a long time. Then I went back to ours.

Amrita's temperature remained the same the next day. The superintendent called a doctor. The diagnosis – measles.

'Oh my God, oh my God,' said the superintendent wringing her hands. 'Now everyone in the hostel will get it. She had better leave the hostel.'

'She has nowhere to go,' I said.

She gave me a look of pure hatred and left the room hurriedly. Half an hour later I was summoned to her office where the principal had joined her. 'What is this I hear?' the principal asked me.

'All what?'

The principal looked at me in amazement and then spoke to me for ten minutes on the subject of respect for elders. Subsequently she expressed her outrage that Amrita had no local guardians in Delhi who could take her away, and her deeper outrage that I couldn't ask my local guardians to look after her. She ordered the superintendent to send a telegram to Amrita's parents in Bangalore. In the meantime Amrita and I were to have our meals in our room. On no account were we to enter the dining-hall. To attend classes, we were to use the back door of the hostel. It would be opened especially for us.

The superintendent placed a call to Amrita's parents but could not get through. She sent a telegram but there was no response. For a week Amrita stayed confined to our room. I continued attending classes, leaving through the back door of the hostel. For some unaccountable reason, it did not matter to them if I infected the others in class, but the dining-room was taboo. Amrita wept silently throughout, and when she was asleep, I did. Often I would wake up at night to find Amrita awake, gazing at the ceiling, her face now full of spots, her large eyes swollen and red. We hardly spoke. Finally the superintendent got through to Amrita's parents. They said they would fly to Delhi the next day. Turning to the wall, Amrita said, 'This is the end. My father will have nothing to do with me. Where will I go? Where will I go?' I could offer no comfort, no sanctuary. I kept saying, 'He won't do that, he won't do that.' Then I said, 'Rakesh is there, he'll see you through, he'll have to.' She was silent and then said, 'Call him, tell him.'

The hostel phone was out of order again. I asked the superintendent if I could use hers. She refused. In the end I walked out of the college gates, my pocket full of fifty paisa coins, while Patram followed me, calling, 'Hemlathaji, come back, come back, I'll report you to the superintendent, I'll tell the principal, you will see what I will do, you will see what happens.' He followed me to the gate and watched me walk to the taxi-stand. The taxiwallas stared at me while I dialled Rakesh's number at his engineering college. I got a wrong number the first time. The second time the call got disconnected. The third time I got through. Rakesh was out, I was told, but would be back in ten minutes. I waited, while the taxiwallas eyed me. One lay down on the charpoi next to me. 'It is so hot,' he groaned. He removed his banyan, lowered his pyjamas and looked at me. I looked away.

It was growing dark and every emerging shadow seemed khaki-clad and wore a wide grin. I walked down the road slowly. Five minutes. A cyclist swerved towards me and I stepped back. He groaned and cycled away rapidly. I walked back and tried the number again. I got through. Rakesh was back. I told him what I could and he said he would be there immediately. I walked a slight distance away from the taxi-stand and waited. 'Madam,' said a voice behind me. I shuddered and looked back. It was the same taxiwalla. He looked me over and scratched his groin. 'Can I help you in any way?' 'No,' I said and turned away. He remained where he was. 'Do you need any fifty paisa coins?' 'No,' I said, 'No.' I walked further away. He followed me. I crossed the road. He stood opposite, staring at me. Ten minutes later Rakesh's motor-cycle came to a halt beside me. The taxiwalla walked back.

Rakesh was in a state of shock and incomprehension. He would sell his motorcycle and pay for the abortion, he declared hoarsely. He would protect her from her parents. He would leave college. As I tried to calm him down, a familiar khaki-clad apparition emerged silently from the shadows and stood before us, grinning.

For the third time Patram escorted me back to the superintendent's office. The principal was there too. It was girls like me who ruined the reputation of the college – breaking rules, making boyfriends, smoking, she said. I didn't smoke, I replied. The principal snorted. Next I would say I didn't have a boyfriend. She pulled the telephone towards her. She was going to phone my local guardians to take me away. I could start packing my things.

I wish I could say at this point that I had let her phone them. I wish I could say that I had walked out of the room with an appropriate remark. I wish I could say that I had told them what I thought of them. Even today I relive that scene and say all that I did not at that time. I wish I didn't have to say that I began to cry hysterically while they watched me with satisfaction. That I begged them to give me another chance. That I told them my parents would never understand. That I kept repeating, please, please don't expel me, I'll never repeat my mistakes. That the superintendent said she wanted all this in writing. That I gave her a written apology, still sobbing, still begging. They both smiled and shook their heads. And the principal asked the superintendent, 'So you think she has realised?' And the superintendent replied, 'Who knows with these girls, they are such good actresses.' And I said, (oh God), I said, 'I will do anything you want me to do, but please don't expel me, please forgive me, please forgive me.' And they said, 'We cannot give you an answer now, we shall have to think about it. We will watch your behaviour and then we will decide.' And I thanked them.

The next morning, from our first floor window, I saw Rakesh's figure next to his motorcycle, waiting outside the gate. I sent him a note through my next-door neighbour, explaining the situation, but he continued waiting in the afternoon sun while I helped Amrita pack her belongings. Her parents arrived in the evening. Her father waited in the superintendent's office while her mother came up to our room and sat next to her daughter, stroking her hair. 'My poor baby,' she said, 'my poor, poor child.' And she smiled at me and said, 'Hemu, beti, thank you for looking after her all this time. My daughter is lucky to have such a friend.' She continued stroking Amrita's hair. 'Ma,' Amrita said, 'Ma, I'm pregnant.' Her mother's hands stopped. 'Ma,' Amrita said, grasping her thigh, 'I'm three months' pregnant Ma. Ma, where will I go? Where will I go?' Her mother was still, so still. She closed her eyes and whispered, 'Bhagwan, hai Bhagwan.'

In the distance a clock struck six. From my position at the window I could see Rakesh outside the gate, waiting.

'*Ma!*'

We started. Amrita's voice sounded strange.

'Ma, I think I'm bleeding.'

She was. Slowly, the white sheets were staining. Amrita began to cry, loud, harsh sounds. Fascinated, I watched the white sheets turning red while the room filled with the horrible sound, till I thought it would have to burst open to let out what it could not possibly contain. And then there was a knock on the door and the superintendent entered. I threw a bedcover over Amrita and her sounds stopped abruptly. The superintendent's eyes bulged. 'What is the matter?'

Amrita's mother began stroking her hair again. 'My daughter is tired. It has been a strain. Please call a taxi. We must leave now.' The superintendent eyed us suspiciously. She came closer to Amrita and whipped the bedcover away. Amrita's mother gasped. The superintendent gave a strangled scream. Amrita closed her eyes and the superintendent said, 'I should have known.'

'Please call a taxi,' her mother said.

'Taxi – nothing doing, I'm calling the principal.' She rushed out of the room and we heard her heavy footsteps echoing down the corridor.

'Beti,' her mother's face was distorted, 'Please call a taxi.'

'I can't, I can't, I'll be expelled. You call one from outside the gate, I'll stay with her.'

'Ma, don't leave me,' Amrita moaned.

I held her hands tightly. 'I'm here.'

Small, incoherent sounds escaped her mother's throat. She looked at us and then went out rapidly.

I was with Amrita for fifteen minutes while she continued bleeding. I used up all the sheets we had to use below and between her. The blood soaked through them all, right down to the mattress, and the room was heavy with its smell. Amrita moaned and twisted and turned and held on to my hand until I felt I could no longer bear the pain of it all. Then the superintendent entered the room with the principal. The principal took the scene in and hit her forehead with her hand.

'Tell her parents to take her away,' she told me. 'Tell them she cannot come back to this college. Where are they?'

'Her mother's gone to get a taxi.' I was shivering violently.

I heard footsteps in the corridor and her mother entered the room, panting. She ignored the superintendent and the principal. 'Beti,' she told me, 'help me carry her down.'

'And don't bring her back,' the principal said, tight-lipped. 'We don't want such girls here.'

'Madam, madam,' the superintendent said hysterically, 'it isn't my fault – she broke the rules and got into this mess.'

They called Patram to carry her suitcases down, while her mother and I carried Amrita downstairs to the waiting taxi, past the superintendent's room, past her amazed father, followed by the principal and the superintendent. We laid Amrita down on the back seat of the taxi and her mother said to me, 'Come with me, beti, please come with me.'

'Nothing doing,' the principal said, holding my arm. 'This girl is going nowhere. We have had enough trouble. Now Amrita is your responsibility.' I stood between them, helpless.

'Will someone tell me what is happening?' her father asked.

'Yes, I will tell you,' the principal said. 'Your daughter is pregnant and at this moment she is aborting. You do what you want with her and don't bring her back to this college.'

Her father's face seemed to shrink. He shook his head uncomprehendingly. Her mother took his arm gently and opened the door of the taxi. 'Get inside,' she said, 'we have to go to the hospital.' She sat at the back with Amrita. Slowly, the taxi drove away.

'So, Hemlathaji,' said the superintendent, but I walked away, away from her, away from the hostel, away from it all, towards the college building. I climbed up the stairs to the first floor and sat there, against the wall.

Much later I looked at my watch. It was 9.45 pm. They would lock the hostel door at 10.00. I walked back slowly and went upstairs to our room. The stench of blood greeted me, and on the bed, an accumulation of sheets, all red and white. I bolted the door and walked to the window. He was still there. I drew the curtains.

The rest, I heard from my mother's sister in Bangalore, who is a good friend of Amrita's mother. She stayed with us for a week and, in the strictest of confidence, gave us a blow-by-blow account of everything. Amrita was in hospital for a day and then flew back with her parents to Bangalore. The following month she was married off. 'That is *luck*,' my aunt said. '*Such* a nice boy, you cannot imagine. So fair, *so* handsome and on top of that, the *only* son. And the wedding . . . what a wedding! She wore a lahenga studded with *real* pearls.' I asked, 'Isn't she going to complete her BA?' My aunt replied, 'What will she do with a BA now? And anyway, her father forbade it. He was a broken man. Do you know, his hair turned grey overnight? Poor man,' she sighed. My mother turned to me. She said, 'I cannot believe you were friendly with a girl like that. You act as though she did nothing wrong. I hope she hasn't influenced you. You'll never understand what a mother goes through till you become a mother. It is my only prayer to God these days, that you make the correct decisions, that you know right from wrong, that you do not go astray.'

Rakesh came to visit me the following term. I told him about Amrita. At the end he said, 'I see.' That is all.

The rules in the hostel became stricter. Patram kept a strict eye on me. Like the Cheshire cat his grin followed me everywhere.

The year I graduated, Amrita wrote. She had no time for letter-writing, she said, at least not for the kind she wished to write to me. There had been too much to cope with that first year – the abortion, her marriage, her first child. And the second year, her second child. So much for Dr Kumar's advice on contraception! she said. Her father began speaking to her after her son was born. Her mother never referred to what happened. But she stood by her.

Of course, her husband knew nothing. He's nice, she said, and also tall and fair and by that definition, they say, handsome. He's all set to groom our sons to be good IAS officers like him, extending his dreary dreams of all that is proper, permanent and powerful. Work was taking her husband abroad the following year. She would probably accompany him. She asked if I could come and stay with her for a while, for more than a while, whenever possible. She longed to talk to me, letters were so difficult. And all the interruptions, babies crying, meals to be cooked . . . you know how it can be, she said. Oh, Hemu, no, you cannot know. Not yet, not yet. She asked, remember Chachaji? He got it all right, didn't he? He will always get it right, won't he? For this is how it will always be, yes, this is how it will always be. Oh, Hemu, Hemu, my stars have changed, haven't they?'

And mine, Amrita, and mine.

When Anklets
Tinkle

———————◆———————

Mr Aggarwal chuckled. 'Madrasis, they are speaking such badly pronouncing English.'

'Yes,' Mr Singh guffawed. 'These Yannas, they are saying yex for x, yam for am . . . when they are speaking English, no one is understanding.'

'How it matters what English they are speaking?' Mr Srivastava groaned. 'All I am wanting is good Madrasi tenant for my barsati and only tenants I am getting are from north.'

The three men were relaxing in the Srivastavas' house on a hot summer day, drinking nimbupani and commiserating over the fact that the Srivastavas' barsati was still unoccupied, three months after he had bought the house. South Indian tenants seemed to have vanished, sucked into the summer loo. The Srivastavas had specially advertised their barsati on the weekend, specifying that it was available for a nice, simple, decent Madrasi boy. But no South Indians were forthcoming. Instead, Punjabi boys, UP boys, boys from MP, Bihar and Bengal arrived at his doorstep and were turned away.

'It is the irony of fate,' Mr Srivastava moaned. 'Punjabi tenant is never vacating any house, is always demanding and fighting and not agreeing to rent being raised.'

Mr Singh nodded sympathetically. 'I myself being Punjabi am seeing this. We Punjabis are not taking nonsense from anybody, Srivastavaji. And that is proving great problem for landlords.'

65

'As for Biharis,' Mr Srivastava sighed, 'they are lazy buggers. Not even having energy to write out cheque for rent.'

'And Banias,' roared Mr Aggarwal, slapping his thigh, 'they are always being stingy.'

'What about Bengali?' Mr Singh asked. 'Bengali boys very nice, very quiet.'

Mr Srivastava shuddered and folded his hands. 'Bengali boys nice as long as their temper not disturbed. Once these Bengalis get angry, they are setting fire to first thing they see. Always they carry matches for such times. I am not wanting to get on wrong side of Bengali. You see how they are setting fire to football stadium in Calcutta every year? That is why stadium is made of wood. One year one side loses and setting fire to it, and next year other side loses and setting fire to it. Thank you, Singhji, no Bengali tenant.'

'Bengalis having culture,' Mr Singh said wistfully.

'I am not wanting culture,' Mr Srivastava said firmly. 'I am wanting down to earth, simple, decent man who pays rent every month and goes when I say go.'

'Madrasi.'

'Yes, Madrasi.'

Mr Aggarwal began to chuckle again. 'Oh these Madrasis are speaking such comical English. Murdering English language. Still, they are most decent tenants. If you raise rent, they are paying; if you are telling them go, they go. Good people, Madrasis.'

'Very intelligent,' Mr Singh added. 'In every school and college Madrasi topping.'

'Very sharp,' agreed Mr Aggarwal. 'Though they are speaking comical English, they are writing top quality English. Now we, we are speaking good English but writing is not so good.'

The electricity went off and the conversation petered off. Soon Mr Aggarwal and Mr Singh took leave of Mr Srivastava, assuring him that they would do all they could to find him a Madrasi tenant.

In the kitchen, Mrs Srivastava sighed, tied her jooda into a tighter knot, dug the hairpin in and felt the sweat trickle down her back and neck as she stirred the kadhi. God knew how long the power cut would last. She had listened to every word of the conversation between her husband and his friends. All talk, she thought. All these men could do was talk. Three months and still no tenant. Her husband had retired a year ago and they had bought this house with their precious savings and a huge loan. Where were they to get the money to pay off the loan without a tenant? And all he did was talk . . . expound on South Indians and Bengalis and God knows who else. When did *she* get to retire? Was there ever any retirement from cooking and cleaning?

Ramsaran, their servant of twenty years, chopped the onions, looking sympathetically at Mrs Srivastava as her brow grew darker. He knew all her moods. Sahib was a spiritual man, he told her comfortingly. Why did she force him to think of mundane things like finding a tenant? Sahib was a man of God, look how often he prayed, and at what length. It was below the good sahib's dignity to turn his mind to such considerations.

Yes, yes, she had heard all that before, Mrs Srivastava snapped, it was convenient being a man of God. She stopped. She hated herself at moments like this when even a servant could bring out her resentment. Like vomit, she thought, it came out like vomit at times like this. There was no stopping it.

Memsahib was also a good woman, Ramsaran went on. Memsahib had been like a mother to him since sahib got him from the village twenty years ago, and he a frightened ten-year-old boy. She had even taught him to read and write. Sahib and memsahib were his Devtas, his Gods. Memsahib should not worry, all would be well.

Mrs Srivastava let out a big sigh. The electricity returned and the table fan began to whirr, and with that, she felt her body cool and her anger suddenly leave. 'Lunch is ready,' she called out to her husband.

Rao arrived with the monsoon, a tall, dark man (just like Lord Krishna, all Mrs Srivastava's friends whispered excitedly) with a smile that melted her completely. It was, in fact, the first day of the monsoon. What rain rain rain. What thunder, what lightning, what an overflow of children screaming with delight as they soaked themselves in that first deluge, what a fleet of little white boats floating and dancing down the drains and puddles. The koyal sang with abandon and Mr Srivastava's craving for pakodas could not be contained. As Mrs Srivastava dropped the first pakoda into the kadhai, there was a knock on the door. It was Mr Singh, holding on triumphantly to this tall man with eyelashes that a girl would envy. Both were soaked under their umbrellas.

'I am bringing you Madrasi tenant, Srivastavaji,' Mr Singh beamed, and entered.

Yes, that was how it had all begun, Mr Srivastava recalled much later. That was how it had all begun.

Mrs Srivastava gave Mr Singh and Rao clean towels and after they had dried themselves as best as they could, they sat down to tea and pakodas. Rao's hair was wonderfully dishevelled. Mrs Srivastava approvingly noted that he smelled clean, had long, sensitive fingers and clean fingernails. A button was missing from his shirt. The poor boy.

Rao was working in the same company as Mr Singh, and Mr Singh recommended him strongly. '*Very* decent man.'

'So,' said Mr Srivastava, 'you are Madrasi.'

'I am from Karnataka.'

'Same thing, same thing. We are liking Madrasis.'

'Actually,' Rao said apologetically, 'Madrasi isn't the correct word. South Indian would be more appropriate.'

Mr Srivastava stared at him.

Rao continued. 'Calling all South Indians Madrasis is like calling all North Indians Punjabis.'

Mr Singh began to chuckle. 'Rao here has hit nail on head.'

Mr Srivastava said, 'For you, because you are Madrasi and Madrasis good tenants, we are asking fifteen hundred rupees only for our beautiful barsati.'

'But your barsati is haunted,' Rao said.

'Haunted!' Mr Srivastava exclaimed. 'What are you saying?'

'Don't you know? Haven't you heard?'

'We are hearing nothing.'

Rao told them. Eight years ago, a young, South Indian girl had lived in the barsati. One day, as quietly as she had lived, she had hung herself. A sweet, gentle girl, no one understood it. Since then, her spirit was said to haunt the barsati. A number of people who had lived in the neighbourhood eight years ago were willing to testify that after midnight, strange sounds began . . . anklets tinkling, bangles clinking, sarees sighing and the sound of low weeping . . . sad, so infinitely, infinitely sad. But there was no reason to be afraid, Rao told his bemused audience, no reason at all. For she was a gentle ghost, and harmless, as she had been when she was alive. In fact, she was a distant cousin of his, known for her kind ways, and this was how he knew the whole story. This was why he had been initially reluctant to consider living in the barsati when Mr Singh recommended it to him. He himself wasn't inclined to believe in ghosts . . . still, at night one tended to get superstitious.

'I am not believing in these things,' Mr Srivastava said uncertainly.

Mrs Srivastava, her hands cold with fear, nodded.

'I too would not like to believe in them,' Rao replied, 'but with these things, who can say? Anyway, can I see the barsati?'

They went upstairs. Two small rooms and a smaller kitchenette. One room opened out on to the terrace. 'Where you can sleep in the summer,' Mr Srivastava said.

They went down. 'It's only this ghost business that bothers me,' Rao said, shaking his head.

Mrs Srivastava came to the point. 'How much you are willing to pay?'

'Seven hundred rupees,' Rao said, suddenly firm. Mr Singh gasped.

'What you are saying!' Mrs Srivastava exclaimed.

'Srivastavaji, I cannot afford any more, and under the circumstances, I think it is a good sum of money. However, if you are not agreeable, I will look elsewhere.'

Mrs Srivastava took over. 'We are willing to negotiate. What you say to six hundred rupees?'

'Fine,' replied Rao promptly.

Mr Srivastava wanted to ask him if now he had no fear of haunted houses, but decided against it. A low paying tenant was better than no tenant. Instead, he observed, 'You are speaking Queen's English. For Madrasi, that is very good.'

'Rao has been to England,' Mr Singh said proudly.

Mr Srivastava looked at him with new respect. 'How that is?'

'My father was in the foreign service.'

'You are liking it there?'

'Well,' said Rao slowly, 'not really. The British still believe that the sun hasn't set on the British Raj.'

'Kindly repeat, I am not understanding.'

'He is saying that the British are thinking they are still the greatest,' Mrs Srivastava said grimly.

Rao smiled. 'Exactly.'

'My daughter,' said Mrs Srivastava, 'who is working as engineer in Madras, she is saying that these British, they are still writing same old stories about India, same, same old stories.'

'Your daughter is absolutely right,' replied Rao.

'My daughter,' said Mrs Srivastava, 'is saying that these English people, they are always writing about killing tigers, or about ruling stupid Indians, or about how India is poor and stinking.'

'True,' said Rao. 'That is all they want to hear, that is all they are willing to read or publish.'

'My daughter, she is saying that with these British, either they are glorifying India, or they are going to other extreme. Either they are writing of maharajas and tigers and snake charmers or else they are writing of slums and people shitting in the open.'

Mr Singh and Mr Srivastava looked away in shock.

'Fine speech you are giving,' Mr Srivastava said, his ears red.

Mrs Srivastava was breathless. She reached out and patted Rao's cheek. 'Beta,' she said, 'so long it is since I am talking like this with anyone.'

'You must be very close to your daughter.'

Mrs Srivastava's eyes suddenly filled with tears. 'Yes. But she is engineer in Madras and is having no leave to come and see her poor mother. And my son, Nikhil, who is doctor, is coming home even less.'

Mr Srivastava who had been brooding, suddenly said, 'I am not agreeing with you. When British here, everything was better. British people were being just, fair and honest. Look at corruption and unrest in this country now.'

'There is unrest in England too,' Rao said.

'Yes, yes!' Mrs Srivastava exclaimed. 'You are right. And then, was it not corrupt of those white skins to rule us? Wearing their coats and ties in the summer and telling us what to do?'

'So,' asked Mr Srivastava belligerently, 'if they are wearing coats and ties in our summer, how that is making them bad?'

70

'That is not making them bad, that is making them foolish. Ruling our country is making them bad. Having separate compartments for whites and Indians in trains is making them bad. Killing Indians when Indians peacefully protesting is making them bad. What you are saying about British fairness!'

Mr Srivastava got up. 'I am going for my puja. You settle lease and all that. Namaste.'

Rao got up. 'Namaste, and thank you.'

Rao settled down nicely. Mrs Srivastava insisted on feeding him for a week till he had his place settled. She tentatively asked him about the spirit. Rao admitted having heard sounds at night but assured her that it was safe. It was, he was sure, a harmless spirit. Wasn't he ever afraid? Sometimes, Rao confessed, but one had to overcome one's fears. She asked him if he had ever seen anything. He replied that it was of no consequence, he did not want her to be afraid. He looked so helpless and vulnerable saying this that she gathered eight shirts from his bed and said that she would sew on the missing buttons.

The neighbours loved Rao, especially the women. They called him Krishna Kannhaiyya and when he told them that he occasionally played the flute, they giggled with delight. Did he not have a Radha, they asked coyly. But Rao only smiled.

It was Ramsaran who made the ghost a reality. A month after Rao's arrival, he informed Mrs Srivastava that the barsati was indeed haunted. For two nights in succession he had heard the tinkle of anklets and the clinking of bangles in Rao's barsati. Once he had heard the strange high-pitched sound of the ghost's laugh. It could not be borne. Ramsaran's dark face was darker now with fear and resentment as he said that it was only his loyalty to them that was keeping him here. It was only his undying gratitude to sahib for giving him a job, that was preventing him from fleeing. He didn't have enough work, Mrs Srivastava responded nervously. Since her children had got jobs and left the house, he spent all his time imagining things. No need to dwell on ghosts. Thwarted, Ramsaran retreated to the back door of the kitchen where he furiously smoked a beedi. Then he returned. Why didn't she believe him? With six small children and one more on the way, did memsahib expect him to work below a haunted house? If the ghost strangled the children at night, what would memsahib and sahib do? If it strangled him, who would look after his wife and children? Would they? Would they?

Quiet, roared Mr Srivastava, emerging from his puja room. Couldn't a man pray in peace? He had had enough of Ramsaran's bak-bak. He banged the door to the room shut and stared accusingly at his Gods.

In the kitchen Mrs Srivastava comforted Ramsaran. If he left them, what would they do, she said, lighting the gas as he kneaded the dough for the chappatis. Leave? Ramsaran echoed, affronted and glowering. How could she say such a thing? For twenty years, since he was a child and sahib got him from the village, he had been with them. He had looked after their children, cleaned her son's bottom, watched them grow up, was waiting to see them married with children of their own. She insulted him by asking him to stay. Where would he go? They were his only family. His own children were secondary, his wife was secondary. She and sahib were his true parents. Ramsaran's voice shook as he briskly wiped a tear from his right eye and began rolling the chappatis. Memsahib shouldn't insult him like this. Would a child desert his parents?

Overwhelmed, ridden with guilt, Mrs Srivastava said that, of course, a child would not, and certainly, she was sure of his loyalty.

But, Ramsaran continued, slapping the chappati angrily on the tawa, what if his own children were strangled by the ghost? Did memsahib have no concern for the little ones?

That wouldn't happen, Mrs Srivastava replied weakly. Ghosts did not exist.

What was she saying? Memsahib knew nothing. He himself had seen a ghost in his village. He was sensitive to spirits and could sense the presence of the one upstairs. Sahib and memsahib were putting his love and loyalty to them through a great test. It was most trying. He feared that he was now falling ill, terribly ill, he could feel it in his bones. He had been shivering all morning, yes, in this heat he had been shivering, he could not possibly come to work the next day, possibly the next few days, even working now was an effort, but he would do it, yes, he would do it for them. *He* was not the person to let them down.

Mrs Srivastava sighed softly. Yes, it was time for Ramsaran's annual illness. Every year, in addition to a month's annual leave, Ramsaran 'fell ill' – hibernated, as it were, in his servant's quarter, and did not emerge for a month or two. He would then send his wife to the house, and she would arrive, small and pretty, anklets tinkling, always giggling and always pregnant. Yes, it was time for his annual hibernation, and he would come out of this smelling of Lifebuoy soap, ready to spring-clean the house, and jealous of the niche his wife had carved for herself. Sita's mother, as his wife was referred to after her first-born, was used to this, and departed, still giggling, payals tinkling, ready to return the following year. And Ramsaran, amidst a clatter of dishes and brooms, would moan how dirty the house had become in his absence. Sita ki amma knew nothing about the house, how she had let it fill with dirt in his absence. Once, Mrs Srivastava replied that his wife was a far more scrupulous cleaner than him and kept the house like a woman should. That night, Ramsaran went to his quarter, got drunk, and soundly thrashed his wife. She came to the Srivastavas' house that night, weeping loudly, followed by four children, also crying. They had done her a great injustice, she sobbed to the horrified Srivastavas, by praising her to her husband. She held out her bruised arms to them. Look, she told them, this is what their appreciation had got her from her husband. Ramsaran was summoned from his quarter. He stood with his head bowed as Mr Srivastava shouted abuse at him. He could leave right now, Mr Srivastava said. He was no longer needed in the house. Did he understand? Ramsaran burst into loud tears and fell at Mr Srivastava's feet. Sita ki amma fell at Mrs Srivastava's feet. If they dismissed her husband, where would they go, who would feed the children? Mr Srivastava flung his hands up in despair. Enough, he had had enough. They had interrupted his puja and he had no time to deal with such fools. He went back to his room, slammed the door and resumed his prayers. Mrs Srivastava comforted them both, lectured Ramsaran and warned him of dire consequences if he did such a thing again. They both touched her feet and departed, followed by the four frightened children, clutching the toffees she had given them.

And now, after dinner, Mrs Srivastava brought up the subject of the errant ghost with her husband. Suppose Rao left? Who then would want to live in a haunted barsati? How would they pay off their loan? Mr Srivastava replied that what would happen would happen. She should trust in God. He would have a puja in the barsati and that would get rid of the spirit if there was one. A sound of great anger emerged from Mrs Srivastava's throat. Where had all his prayers got them all these years, she burst out. Did his prayers get the seven hundred rupees a month that helped pay for their children's college? While he prayed, she had tutored the children, managed the house, worked as a schoolteacher, and *saved*, yes, saved – saved enough to partly pay for this house, this *haunted* house. The one decision to buy a house she had left to him, and even that he had messed up. His prayers had kept him in ignorance; in ignorance of her suffering, in ignorance of her pain, in ignorance of the injustice of it all. Large tears rolled down Mrs Srivastava's plump face. Her husband replied that he was tired of her nagging and he was going to his room for his puja. Go, she told him, he could go to his Gods and take refuge with them. And Mr Srivastava went to his Gods and prayed and meditated for two hours.

The next morning, Sita ki amma arrived, all smiles. *He* was ill, she told Mrs Srivastava, so here she was. Mrs Srivastava clicked her tongue – she was pregnant again? What number was this one? Sita ki amma giggled. Seventh, she whispered and began peeling the garlic. Mrs Srivastava shook her head in exasperation. She should never have let her and her family stay here during the Emergency, she told Sita ki amma. They looked at each other and began to laugh. Ten years ago, during the Emergency, when forced sterilisations were at their peak, a truck arrived at the servant's quarters, filled with Youth Congress zealots. They chased and picked up all the males in the vicinity, aged fifteen to eighty, bundled them into the truck, and drove them to the Government hospital to be sterilised. Ramsaran, his wife and three girls (still three then) came panting to the Srivastavas. If memsahib and sahib didn't hide them, it would be the end. The prospect of no sons and lost virility had reduced Ramsaran to near hysteria, while Sita ki amma sobbed and giggled alternately. Mrs Srivastava cleared a room for them in the house where they stayed for a week. By then the Youth Congress had proceeded to the neighbouring colonies and Sita ki amma was pregnant again. When the fifth child was on its way, Mr Srivastava told Ramsaran that he should have let the Youth Congress have its way with him. Why didn't he get himself operated on now at least? After all, he did have one son. Ramsaran was most indignant. Did sahib want him to become impotent, lose his manhood? Children were God's gift to him and if he was willing to look after them, then who was sahib to say anything? Mr Srivastava told him to hold his tongue; from whom did he borrow huge sums of money every month to feed his brood of children? Ramsaran promptly fell ill the next day and that was the end of that.

Now, Mrs Srivastava advised Sita ki amma to have herself operated on when the child was born. Sita ki amma agreed but said that she would have to do it without *his* knowledge. And on no account was memsahib to let *him* know.

That very night, their daughter, Namita, arrived, soaked to the skin. She had sent them a telegram announcing her arrival but it hadn't arrived. (It arrived the next day.) Mr Srivastava bemoaned the fact that he hadn't been able to meet his child at the station and damned the telegraph service, damned the rain. He began heating milk for her while his wife hugged Namita and cried. She had become thinner, they noted, had dark circles beneath her eyes and her collar-bones showed. But she was here for a month! Bliss. Bliss. Mrs Srivastava said a quick prayer of thanks before her husband's Gods and Mr Srivastava let the milk boil over as he gazed at his daughter with tenderness. It is only for you that he will boil milk, Mrs Srivastava told Namita as she cleaned the gas range, and even that he won't do properly. After Namita changed, they sat by her and watched her towelling her hair, listened as she told them about her journey and her work. She had bought two sarees for her mother and two shirts for her father. Mrs Srivastava told her husband that after all these years she was finally getting what he had never given her. Finally, she was being indulged. Mr Srivastava replied that even he was finally being indulged. And who, asked his wife, made pakodas for him every evening? Namita told them both to stop it.

Early next morning Mr Srivastava went to the market to buy chicken, mangoes and jamun. Mrs Srivastava and Sita ki amma cooked in a frenzy. Then they watched, agonised, as Namita picked at her food. Too thin, too thin, Sita ki amma told Mrs

Srivastava, no flesh on her cheeks, on her breasts, on her hips. How would she ever become a mother? Sita ki amma was a fine one to talk, Mrs Srivastava retorted, when she was half Namita's size and the mother of almost seven. In the evening the neighbours dropped in with home-made gulab jamuns, pedas, dahi vadas and more jamuns and mangoes from their own trees. Eat, child, eat, they urged the laughing, protesting Namita. She was too thin. She needed to fill out. Having no flesh was fashionable, but she looked like she had jaundice. Wasn't she planning to get married? It was all very well to be an engineer, but marriage was a must. How old was she? Twenty-seven, said Namita. Twenty-four, said her mother simultaneously, but more loudly. Well then? Twenty-four was a good age to get married. They would find another engineer for her. Or would a doctor be preferable? Would she like a doctor in England or America? India was no longer the place to be in. She should go abroad and make money. Abroad she would have true job satisfaction. Too much bureaucracy in India, too much red tape. And if she had a baby, the child would have foreign citizenship and *so* many more opportunities than in India. Well? Well?

She didn't want to marry yet. No? No. She was quite happy as she was. She certainly didn't want to go to England. In fact, marriage wasn't necessary. Not necessary? Mrs Srivastava, what was the child saying!

One of the neighbours saw Rao outside and hailed him from the window. Rao strolled in and was introduced to Namita. How nice her Nami was looking, Mrs Srivastava thought fondly. The magenta saree brought out the best in her, highlighted her large eyes and long black hair, even if she did look too thin. For a brief moment, Rao's eyes seemed to reflect what she felt, then he turned his attention to the plate she had filled with snacks. Namita watched him as he happily consumed it all. Such a nice boy, the neighbours told her, and that too, staying in a haunted house! To Namita's puzzled look, they responded with the story of the sad spirit. Rao, they said, was such a good man, so fond of her mother that he was willing to stay there in spite of this. Mrs Srivastava gave Rao an affectionate look. Namita threw him a sharp glance and saw him looking sheepish.

'How interesting,' Namita said. 'Do tell me more about the ghost.'

Rao smiled and shrugged his shoulders. 'Nothing to tell, really.'

'He isn't wanting to scare your poor mother,' Mrs Srivastava said indulgently.

Rao looked away.

'You believe in ghosts?' Namita persisted.

'But beti, of course,' a neighbour said. 'Even we are hearing sounds of bangles and all that at night. Are you not also hearing, Raoji?'

Rao shrugged again. 'I'm a sound sleeper.'

'And an accomplished one,' Namita said dryly. Her mother looked at her in astonishment. How rude her Nami's tone was. What was wrong with the girl?

'Rao here,' Mrs Srivastava said, trying to make up, 'is travelling all over the world.'

'Did you encounter ghosts in your travel abroad too?'

Rao began to smile slowly. 'Yes, all kinds.' He got up. 'If you'll excuse me, I have to leave.' He folded his hands, gave a charming smile and left.

'He is sweetest boy,' sighed a neighbour.

After everyone left, Namita lost her temper. Did they realise what a fool he had made of them? Haunted house indeed. She thought her parents were *educated* people. Did they know how he had taken advantage of them? Fools, fools. Mrs Srivastava told her not to dare call them that. But they *were*, her daughter said, they were. Giving him that place for much less than it was worth because of some ridiculous story about ghosts. Were they so naive that they didn't realise the 'ghosts' were women? Innocent Madrasi indeed. Didn't they realise that he was laughing at their expense? Laughing while consuming one gulab jamun, two pedas and one dahi vada? She counted, said Mrs Srivastava, shocked. Yes, she counted, Namita replied.

But, of course, her father said, it was all her mother's fault. She had clinched the deal. He had never trusted the fellow, never believed the story, but then he was an educated man.

He and she, warned Mrs Srivastava, both had their BAs, so he had better watch his words. What was he capable of doing, besides praying? If they were so concerned, let them find another tenant. Besides, men would be men and if he had girlfriends it was none of their business to interfere.

Very modern she had become, her husband said. But Namita spoke at length of the humiliation of it all, then she began to weep and her mother followed and Mr Srivastava retreated to his room to pray.

The next morning, Mrs Srivastava asked Sita ki amma about the ghost. Sita ki amma buried her head in her hands and shook in a paroxysm of laughter. Finally she said, even you, memsahib. Of course she knew Rao's ghosts were women all along. She had seen them go up to his room and come down too, and they were always laughing. It was all very funny.

Why then had she not told her hysterical husband?

Because it suited her not to tell him. This way he felt God was punishing him for his sins and he didn't get drunk or beat her. The longer he believed in the ghost, the better for her. And the Madrasi was quite discreet; his friends only came to visit him late at night.

She was a fine one, Mrs Srivastava said, suppressing a smile.

He was a truly kind man, Sita ki amma said, stirring the vegetables. He always had sweets for her children and once he had got them all exercise books and pencils for school. Besides no one said anything about Lord Krishna and his hundreds of gopis. And this Madrasi had only two or three.

Namita proved to be less amenable. Even you're charmed by this fraud, she told her mother angrily. He was a grown-up man, her mother said. Double standards, her daughter snapped. If her mother had a female tenant who was visited at night by numerous men, would she be so calm? That wasn't the same thing, her mother replied, but when Namita asked her why she couldn't reply. Enough of your arguments, she told her daughter. She was here for a month and the least she could do was be pleasant. And, Namita continued, that wasn't the point. The point was that her parents were getting seven hundred rupees for a barsati that was worth twice as much. A good tenant was better than no tenant and the subject was closed, her mother said.

A week later Rao came down and told her in Namita's presence that he would begin paying twelve hundred rupees a month the following month onwards, since he had just got a promotion and could now afford it. He was looking at Namita as he spoke to her and it looked as though he was trying hard to suppress his laughter.

Mrs Srivastava patted his cheek. After he left she looked enquir-
ingly at Namita. She had told him, Namita said. Mrs Srivastava's
eyes widened. The previous day, Namita said, she had gone up to
his room and told him that he had no right to have done what he
did. She had gone up to his room, Mrs Srivastava echoed faintly.
Namita let out a sound of exasperation. Her mother had her
priorities all wrong and the subject was closed.

A few days later their neighbours, the Singhs, dropped in, elabor-
ately casual, with their son, Surinder. 'Our son is doctor in
England,' they told the Srivastavas meaningfully. Surinder
shrugged his shoulders modestly. He seemed to be having trouble
with his tie which he kept fingering, and his Harris tweed coat was
making him perspire. 'All from London,' Mrs Singh told the
Srivastavas meaningfully. 'Where you get quality coats like this in
India?'
   'How long you are in England?' Mrs Srivastava asked him,
smiling.
   'Two years I am there,' Surinder replied. His accent was an
interesting mix of Punjabi and British.
   'You are liking it there?'
   Surinder looked unhappy. His mother nudged him. 'Yes, yes,'
he sighed.
   Sita ki amma entered with a trayload of tea and snacks. After
they were served, Mrs Srivastava said, 'What English are thinking
of Indians? How they are treating Indians?'
   Surinder looked sadder. 'Sometimes it is all right. And sometimes they are discriminating.'
   'My daughter,' Mrs Srivastava said proudly, 'she is having many
strong opinions about British.'
   'Yes,' Surinder said, an expression of great gloom descending
on his good-natured features. 'British calling us Indian and Paki
pigs.'
   There was an awkward silence. Mrs Srivastava called, 'Nami,
beti, guests are here.'
   A few minutes later Namita entered the room and greeted them.
Her parents looked at her in some consternation. She was looking
her worst in a pair of old jeans and a faded pink kurta. The Singhs

smiled and introduced her to their son. 'He is doctor in London,' Mrs Singh said proudly. Surinder looked shyly at his shoes.

'Change your clothes, wear a saree,' Mrs Srivastava whispered to Namita. Namita got up and sat next to her father. 'How can you bear to live in that country?' she asked Surinder.

Surinder looked at her as a drowning child might look at its rescuer. 'You are speaking words of great truth,' he said simply.

Namita looked taken aback. 'Are you feeling cold?' she asked. Mrs Srivastava drew in her breath sharply.

Surinder beamed. 'No,' he said and took off his Harris tweed. He then loosened his tie and gazed at Namita adoringly.

'If you'll excuse me,' Namita said, 'I have to leave. Namaste.'

'Surinder, you go with her,' Mrs Singh said, and Surinder rose with alacrity.

'No, no need,' Namita said, throwing her parents a look of fury. 'I'm going to Ramsaran's quarter to see how he's feeling.' Surinder sat down.

After she left Mr Singh said, 'She is good girl. Who these days is showing concern for servants?'

That night Namita lost her temper again. 'Don't matchmake for me,' she told her parents. 'It's humiliating. I'm not on display.'

He was a good boy, her father said, and they knew his parents. They could both work in London. There would be no question of dowry. What more did she want? They were not telling her to give up her career. She should eat another chappati, she was too thin.

And, her mother said, she would be twenty-eight in four months. She should keep an open mind to marriage. The older one got, the harder it was. They were not forcing her to marry, not dragging her to the sacred fire. What was the harm in seeing boys with an open mind? Compatibility was all a question of adjustment, she shouldn't have any illusions about compatibility. Who would look after her after they were dead and gone? If she had found someone of her own choice they would be the first to agree. But she hadn't and how much longer could she wait? As she grew older she was becoming increasingly cantankerous. That's what happened to spinsters. Marriage softened a woman, taught her to adjust, made her aware of what sacrifice meant. She was very selfish and had not an iota of concern for her old, retired parents.

Namita got up. She was going for a walk.

In the kitchen Mrs Srivastava found Sita ki amma convulsed in giggles. Now what was the matter with *her*?

That man. That man they wanted baby to marry was wearing a coat in this heat. Sita ki amma held her stomach, doubled over with laughter. Hai Ram, he was wearing a coat!

And what, snapped Mrs Srivastava, made her think he was meant for Namita?

Did memsahib take her to be a fool? It was so obvious. But he wasn't good enough for baby. Why didn't they marry baby to that nice Madrasi upstairs?

She was mad, Mrs Srivastava said, stirring the boiling milk.

Oh no, she wasn't, Sita ki amma replied. She knew everything. Right now baby was going for a walk with the Madrasi.

What?

They were well suited, better suited than the Punjabi in the coat. Overcome with giggles, she buried her face in her hands.

If she knew so much about men, Mrs Srivastava retorted, why had she married someone like Ramsaran?

Because, giggled Sita ki amma, scrubbing the dishes, she wasn't an engineer.

Namita's holidays were coming to an end. Just a week for his daughter to leave, Mr Srivastava mourned, slowly taking out the jamuns and mangoes from his shopping basket. Now, when he had brought *some* colour into her cheeks, she was going.

Mrs Srivastava walked slowly to the veranda and sat down. Now they would have to wait another nine–ten months to see her, and then too, only for as many days. Ten months anticipating her arrival, ten days dreading her departure. She did not feel this way when her son left, dearly though she loved him. No, she did not feel this way. She watched the drizzle. The worst of the monsoon was over and for once there had been no floods. There would be a good crop this year and hopefully the prices wouldn't rise. Mrs Singh waved to her from the balcony and Mrs Srivastava waved back. Surinder had reluctantly left for Chandigarh to look at some more girls. The Singhs had been so keen on her Nami. She had to make the excuse that Namita didn't want to live abroad. Mr Singh understood, but Mrs Singh was offended. What was wrong with her son? For some time there was coolness between the two women but soon Mrs Singh's natural good nature took over and she came over to the Srivastavas with a tiffin-carrier full of dahi vadas for Namita. She knew that Namita loved dahi vadas and the poor child was leaving in a few days. The problem, Mrs Srivastava thought, was that Surinder had fallen quite madly in love with Namita. Besotted, her daughter said, after receiving several poems from him. Well, nothing could be done about that. He would get over it as everyone in love inevitably did. That Sita ki amma had eyes at the back of her head, she thought. She was right, Namita and Rao had been seeing a lot of each other. Well, that wasn't such a bad thing. Sita ki amma had even informed her that the visiting ghosts had come to a halt. She did not say anything to her daughter. Just don't visit him in his house, she warned her once. It was most unseemly and she didn't want Namita to get a bad reputation. Besides, men, even the best of them, would take this as a sign of a girl's willingness. She herself couldn't gauge the situation. Rao seemed his usual laughing self with Namita and Namita gave no indication of how she felt. Mrs Srivastava noted that Namita always wore her best sarees when she went out with Rao, but her expression was unreadable. Was this just another friend like her male friends in college? How could Rao not love her . . . she had so much love to give, was so fiercely loyal and strong beneath all that temper. Of course, her husband, immersed in his prayers, was oblivious to what was going on. But now Namita was leaving and she didn't have the courage to ask her what was going on.

That night Mrs Srivastava dreamt strange dreams. Rao was having dinner with the ghost. He was laughing and the spirit – such a pretty one – joined him. Oh, she wasn't one to be feared. Suddenly Mrs Srivastava awoke. Looking at her watch, she saw that it was 2 am. She looked at her gently snoring husband. What was it that had woken her? Then she heard sounds from upstairs filtering down to her bedroom window like a gentle drizzle . . . anklets tinkling, bangles clinking and low laughter. Her blood froze. So it was true. Poor Rao. Poor, poor Rao. To live with a ghost and live so uncomplainingly. She shivered. It didn't sound like a sad ghost. They all said it wept, but she could hear it laughing. There. There, she could hear it again, the clink of bangles and soft laughter . . .

then Rao's voice, also laughing softly. Did he then, talk to the ghost?

In the silence that followed, she was suddenly wide awake. Realisation and fear seeped through her like poison. Slowly, she got out of bed. For some time, she stood there, not wanting to know, her heart beating like the heart of a mad woman. She walked to her daughter's room and opened the door. Namita was not there.

Trembling, she sat on the bed. She would wait. She would not go up – no, not that. She would wait.

Two hours later she heard the front door open softly and footsteps coming towards the room. Namita came to the door and stopped. She stood there, her face in the shadows and they looked at each other. Then she entered and sat next to her mother. For five minutes they sat wordlessly and then Mrs Srivastava said, how long. A few days, Namita replied. Had she, her mother asked, and then stopped. There was a long silence and then Namita said, yes.

A sound of deep pain emerged from Mrs Srivastava's throat. Over. All over. It was the end.

Namita said, please don't tell Daddy.

Had she, asked her mother, kept anything from her husband?

Ma, please.

Mrs Srivastava put her hand to her mouth. She would not cry. Did her daughter realise the implications of what she had done?

Namita seemed to have difficulty finding the right words. It could not be explained, she said at last. Her mother would never understand. Never.

What was there to understand, Mrs Srivastava whispered. She had lost control of herself.

She had not, Namita replied, her voice shaking. She knew what she was doing. She had wanted to do it.

Mrs Srivastava thought she would faint.

Namita continued, would her mother react the same way if she were a son? What about her brother, Nikhil? Wasn't her mother aware of his affairs? Why had she never reprimanded him? Nikhil was younger than her. She was not a child. She was sick of this hypocrisy.

Mrs Srivastava gathered her forces. How difficult it was to fight in whispers, she thought. Logic didn't solve the problems in the world, she told Namita. Her daughter might win the argument, but lose everything else. In fact, she had. Did she think Rao would marry her now? Did she think he had any respect for her? Did she –

Yes, Rao wanted to marry her, he wanted to marry her, he wanted to marry her. What about *her*? Did none of them care how *she* felt? What about *her* wanting to marry *him*? What about *that*?

Mrs Srivastava hit her forehead with her hand. It had come to this.

Yes, her daughter hissed. It should have come to this long ago.

What was wrong with Rao, Mrs Srivastava asked.

He wasn't a virgin, Namita replied, then, seeing her mother's expression, said, but that was what was wrong with *her*, wasn't it?

Silently, Mrs Srivastava began to cry, her plump shoulders heaving. There was a sound at the door and her husband stood there, a frail figure in a white pyjama-kurta. What was going on, he asked, aggrieved. It was 4 am in the morning. And why was Namita still in her saree at this ungodly hour?

Mrs Srivastava turned on him like a fury. Couldn't a mother talk to her daughter if she wished? If her daughter was leaving in less than a week, was time any consideration? Couldn't a mother want some time alone with her child? If she chose to talk to her daughter at 4 am what business was it of his? Always interfering, he had always interfered in her life. Always, why, why, why? What was the matter with him? Was he blind to the workings of a mother's heart? He was blind, certainly, to the pain in hers and would he please leave them alone. Mrs Srivastava's tears flowed unabated and she fiercely blew her nose into her saree palla.

Mr Srivastava folded his hands. He was going, pray forgive him for asking such an innocent question, he was going. She was a hysterical woman, all women were hysterical and yes, certainly he would leave. He loved his daughter too but had less neurotic ways of expressing it. He would certainly leave, and they could talk till the sun rose and the cock crowed and the milkman came if they so pleased. He stormed out, leaving the curtains swishing furiously.

Poor Daddy, Namita said.

Poor *Daddy*? *Poor* Daddy! Indeed. *Good*, Daddy, *kind* Daddy, Daddy who bought her her favourite jamuns and mangoes and

chicken, Daddy who was so busy praying that he never reprimanded her for her arrogant ways, never corrected her. The best
father in the world, married to the worst mother. Never, poor
Mummy, who bore the brunt of everything, who disciplined,
scolded, slogged like a servant, no, never never that. Could she
tell *poor* Daddy what she had done? Would he resolve the situation
by praying some more? More likely the shock would send all
prayers out of his mind. Yes, what about poor *Mummy*, forced
into silence and confusion while poor Daddy, blissfully ignorant,
continued indulging his darling daughter? Did she think he would
take it with the equanimity that she had? Did she think he would
ever forgive her?

Namita was quiet until her mother's tears subsided. Then she
put her hand on her mother's. Her hand was wet, her mother
observed. Truly, her daughter was a liberated woman. Was she
pregnant?

If she was, her daughter snapped, it was too soon to know and
she wasn't a fool and would her mother stop it stop it stop it.

As though to reinforce her words, there was a loud banging on
the front door (as though dacoits had come, Mrs Srivastava told
her neighbours later). Mr Srivastava came running to the room
(thinking God knows what had happened to his only daughter –
no concern for her, of course). They ran to the door and heard
Ramsaran's voice, shouting, memsahib, sahib, open, hai Ram,
open! Mr Srivastava unbolted the door and Ramsaran entered,
wailing loudly. His wife was dying, dying, help him, his wife was
dying, dying! He dropped down to the floor, beating his chest, she
was dying. Quiet, roared Mr Srivastava, would he stop wailing
and talk sense? Yes, Ramsaran said, what could he say, who would
look after his six children, how could they live without their
mother? Tonight and the night before, even he had heard the
ghost, heard her clearly and that was the cause of all his recent
troubles, hai Ram, how much more loyalty did they want from
him? Would he and his children have to die before sahib felt
compelled to leave this cursed house?

As Mr Srivastava roared again, Mrs Srivastava and Namita ran
to the servant's quarters. All the servants had gathered outside
Ramsaran's quarter, from where muffled groans emerged. The
baby wasn't coming out, someone told Mrs Srivastava, and Sita ki

85

amma would die. Outside the room the six children huddled together, crying.

Mrs Srivastava told Namita to get her father to start the car while she stayed with Sita ki amma. Namita ran back to the house where Ramsaran, still wailing, had positioned himself at Mr Srivastava's feet, his hands firmly around them. With some difficulty they disengaged him and ran to the garage. The car would not start. She would ask Rao to take his car, Namita said, and before her shocked father could protest, ran upstairs and came down with the pyjama-clad Rao (alone to his room at that time, her daughter had no sense of propriety, he told his expressionless wife later). In a matter of minutes, Rao, Sita ki amma and Mrs Srivastava drove off into the pale sunrise.

'Bloody fool,' Mr Srivastava muttered.

'Poor woman,' Namita murmured.

At lunchtime Rao and Mrs Srivastava returned, the former still in his pyjamas. Sita ki amma had had a baby boy, a Caesarean, after a prolonged and painful labour. Yes, her tubes had been tied up, and she would be discharged in a few days. Already she was giggling faintly. Ramsaran fell first at Mrs Srivastava's feet, and then at Rao's. Gods, they were his Gods. He would be indebted to them in every life. Mr Srivastava told him to have a bath – the whole house was smelling. And he had better feed his children, Mrs Srivastava said, filling the tiffin-carrier with dal, vegetables and rice. Overwhelmed, and scowling fiercely, Ramsaran took the food and left. And Mrs Srivastava sat at the dining-table, her head in her hand, looking at Rao.

Rao traced a pattern on the table-cloth. The laughter had gone from his face and he looked tired. He looked up and said, 'I want to marry Namita. Can you persuade her to agree?'

Mrs Srivastava said nothing. Mr Srivastava in a strangled voice, said, '*My* daughter?' Rao nodded. Mr Srivastava sat opposite his wife. He gazed at his daughter tenderly. 'Why do you need persuasion, my child?'

Namita's face was flushed. 'I need more time to know him.'

Mrs Srivastava shook her head silently. More time to know him after what she had done!

How much was he earning? Mr Srivastava asked Rao. Rao told him. His daughter earned much more, Mr Srivastava said. Rao didn't mind. Of course he didn't mind, Mrs Srivastava said. It was very convenient for him, wasn't it? Besides, he was a year younger than her daughter. That didn't matter, Mr Srivastava said, folding his hands and closing his eyes, even Radha was older than Krishna.

Rao got up and sat next to Mrs Srivastava. 'I am sorry if I have caused you any pain,' he said gently. 'Please forgive me.' Mrs Srivastava looked away.

What pain, Mr Srivastava said, irritated. Every mother had to lose a daughter some time. It was the natural course of things. She should be rejoicing, not sitting around with a swollen face like that. She had better keep her tears for the actual wedding.

She hadn't said yes, Namita interrupted. They were all being very presumptuous.

'Could we go for walk?' Rao asked Namita.

It was a two-hour walk. They were smiling when they returned, Rao's fingers touching Namita's as they walked towards the veranda. Mr Srivastava avoided looking at their brushing hands. Mrs Srivastava rose, and as they stepped on to the veranda, hugged them. She told them to sit outside, then went to the kitchen and emerged, holding a steel plate with some rice and dahi. Stand next to each other, she said. Obediently, they did as she instructed. She dipped a few grains of rice in the dahi and pressed it first, on Rao's forehead, then Namita's. God bless them both, she said. Live long, Mr Srivastava said.

Later, they sat around the dining-table, drinking nimbupani, and Rao said, 'My parents are coming to Delhi in a couple of days. I'll tell them about Namita and would like them to meet you.'

Shock registered on Mrs Srivastava's face. Two days? That gave her no time to prepare things, get the house cleaned, buy sweets, what would Namita wear, all her good sarees were in Madras, would she wear her mother's pink and gold Benarasi saree with the Hyderabadi pearls?

Namita began to laugh. She would wear whatever her mother wanted her to wear.

And, her father said, she would now have to find a job in Delhi.

Oh no, Namita replied. Rao would have to find a job in Madras.

Aghast, Mr Srivastava looked at Rao.

Was that the issue? Mrs Srivastava asked Namita.

That, and a lingering ghost, Namita replied.

Exorcised now, Rao said swiftly.

What was all this? Mr Srivastava asked.

Now onwards, Rao said firmly, he would follow Namita to the ends of the earth. He began to smile.

That night Ramsaran returned to work and cooked an elaborate meal for the prospective son-in-law. That was the least he could do, he said, for the man who had saved his wife's life.

They would have to find another decent Madrasi tenant, Mr Srivastava sighed, eating his third chappati.

Any tenant would do, Mrs Srivastava said. He should stop being so communal.

Anklets tinkling and all that, Mr Srivastava said, shaking his head. Who but a decent Madrasi would put up so quietly with it? Rao choked and Namita began to cough.

They were gone, Rao said, gulping down some water. The ghosts were gone for good.

Ramsaran folded his hands. His prayers had been answered, then. With the birth of his seventh child and Namita-baby's engagement, evil spirits had been exorcised.

It was all God's will, Mr Srivastava said. The ghost had never bothered him. He had got so much peace by praying. He helped himself to a sixth chappati.

Prayers had certainly given him peace, Mrs Srivastava said, but not for the reasons he thought they had. She began cutting the melon.

Ramsaran gave a rare smile as he collected the dishes. Memsahib was very funny.

Rao reached out for a slice of melon, cut it into small pieces and placed them on Namita's plate. Eat some more, he said, putting a piece into Namita's mouth.

Soon Mr Srivastava got up. Time for his puja, he said, rubbing his stomach.

Time for their walk, Namita said, rising with Rao.

Mrs Srivastava walked to the veranda and sat on the chair. What a clear and rain-washed night. She watched her daughter and Rao slowly walking down the road. As they turned the corner Rao put an arm around her daughter. Why, thought Mrs Srivastava, had no one wanted to follow *her* to the ends of the earth? Silly, she was being silly. She heard her husband cough behind her. He could not concentrate on his puja, wasn't that strange? He sighed heavily as he sat behind her. His fledgling was going to fly. His fledgling, Mrs Srivastava replied tartly, had flown years ago. Mr Srivastava gazed unseeingly into the distance. After all these years, he said, some strange man had come and snatched her from them.

The shadow of a smile lit Mrs Srivastava's face as she gently tapped his arm. Silly man . . . he was a silly, silly man.

Incantations

◆

One hot summer night, when I was twelve and tear-deep in Victorian fiction, dreaming in bed beside my sister that I was Jane Eyre and Agnes wooed by Rochester and David, I felt my sister shuddering. It was the eve of her wedding, and I, with all the wisdom of my twelve years, turned to her, and putting my arm around her heaving body, assured her that there was no need for pre-wedding nerves, for wasn't Nikhil, her husband-to-be, kind and tender and handsome, and she, beautiful to boot? Turning to me then, she held my hand in a painful grip and said that two days ago she had been raped by Nikhil's brother, Abhinay. As she put the back of her hand to her mouth to stifle a moan, I moved over to her bed, lay beside her and held her. But the sounds from her throat could not be controlled. Our parents would hear. I helped Sangeeta out of bed to the bathroom, pulled the flush, turned on both taps and shut the bathroom door. She sat on the pot, I on the damp floor, and after ten uncontrolled minutes, she laid her head against the wall, and, turning away from me, spoke.

Nikhil's mother had taken her shopping for sarees two days ago and Abhinay, his younger brother, decided to join them. 'You'll make someone a good husband,' his mother had teased, 'if you have so much patience with women shopping.' And patient he had been. After the shopping he had told his mother that he would drop her, then Sangeeta, home. He dropped his mother and then asked Sangeeta if they could stop briefly at the barsati where he lived, as he had to pick up something. He insisted she didn't stay alone in the car, so she went up with him. Once inside, he locked the door.

My sister, who had been staring at the wall as she spoke, now looked at me. I try now to imagine how I looked to her then, pyjama-clad, thin, hair in a tight plait, my face like the photograph she once took of me, guileless, adoring. My sister turned away from me and said, 'Then he raped me.' I put my hands around her bare feet and held them tightly, leaning my face against her thighs. 'I didn't fight,' she said. 'He said he'd deny it and tell everyone I wanted it. He said no one would believe me. And he took so long over it, so long.' She turned to me and felt my cheek. 'Do you know what rape is?' I made a sound of assent and felt my cheeks wet against her nightie. Yes, I knew what rape was. I wasn't supposed to know, I wasn't even supposed to know what sex is. Relentlessly my friend and I had proceeded to find out, our only source being the books we were not supposed to read. The *Reader's Digest*, though not forbidden, gave us a vague idea, for there was always something about the do's and don'ts of marital strife, the musts and must nots of sexual convolutions. Add excitement to marriage, the *Digest* instructed, do it under the dining-table, on the dining-table, under the bed, in the bathtub. My friend and I sighed with excitement. Oh to be married! Light candles, the *Digest* urged, use perfume, open the door for your husband one evening, naked! My friend and I shivered. Could the excitement in marriage ever cease? Never! Could one ever be done with all these experiments? Impossible! But with all this going on how did married people look so calm, so matter of fact, so unlike the exuberance of the Daily Act? One historic day, my friend discovered a much-thumbed paperback in her parents' room, which, when they were out she read swiftly, terror-stricken at the prospect of their arrival, enthralled at the discoveries she was making. It was rather complicated, she told me later in hushed tones. Sex apparently, was divided into three stages – foreplay, meaning kissing; intercourse, meaning intercourse; climax, meaning some height; and orgasm, meaning some release. The art of kissing, one we had always thought so simple, seemed almost as fraught with complications as the act that followed. The book said it was not confined to the lips and required great expertise. The rest was hazy. We could not put action to any of the words. We pondered over the question of time. Ten minutes? Half an hour? One hour? Furtively we tried to imagine our parents doing it. But no, that was not possible.

Parents were beyond such experiments, beyond such desires, beyond any heights, any releases. Mystified, frustrated, delighted, we stared at each other. It was a far more complex and lengthy process than we had anticipated and, therefore, certainly far more to be desired. Sex was something that one day would happen to the likes of us and then lightning would crack and the heavens would change colour. We would have our Rochesters and our Rhett Butlers, it was only a question of time. A question of time when our noses would become finer, our lips more sensual, our eyes large and liquid, our hair thick and luxurious, the kind men loved to run their fingers through. A question of time before the pimples would vanish gracefully, the breasts appear mysteriously, the hair on our arms and legs fall off quietly, our eyebrows arch and distance themselves silently Only a question of time, of time. Not the times our mothers were subject to, who slept with bedroom doors wide open on beds three feet away from our fathers, who had slept that way ever since we could remember. No, not the time our mothers were subject to, who as brides, were even more ignorant than we were as children I think now of these multitudes of mothers, once silent brides entering yellow and white flower-bedecked bedrooms after the wedding, against which their bridal sarees burnt red and gold. How did our fathers undress these women, so many of whom did not even know the reason for such a ritual? Did our mothers then protest, silently, silently? Or quietly, unprotestingly acquiece to what some instinct told them had to be endured, hearing during the act, like incantations, the distant refrain of their mothers' voices, chanting, do what your husband tells you to, accept, endure. Or perhaps, stricken with shyness and the strangeness of it all, did our fathers speak falteringly to their brides, initiate them slowly, gently, assuming an experience they never had? Was there the possibility for love? And their stories lay untold, swollen like rivers after the monsoon rains. Years later, untold stories still, and our mothers like the parched, cracked countryside, waiting for rain that will never come.

'After raping me,' Sangeeta said, 'he dropped me home.' I recalled that evening, recalled that my mother was busy getting everything arranged for the women's sangeet. The house was decorated with rangoli and the kitchen, redolent with the smell of cooking. Two hours before the sangeet, Sangeeta entered the house and I remembered how strange she looked, her eyes swollen, face pale, her saree more crumpled than the heat warranted. She told our mother that the heat was bothering her and Ma shepherded her to the bedroom and urged her to hurry and get ready. And I remembered that she took two hours over her bath. Then our relatives and friends arrived in a glitter of gold and Kanchivaram sarees. Sangeeta, exquisite in a yellow and silver Benarasi saree with pearls, her hair covered with jasmine, sat mutely as someone played the dholak and everyone sang. As the songs turned sentimental, lamenting the daughter leaving her mother's house, my mother, predictably, began to cry, but Sangeeta, playing with the gold bangles on her wrist, did not. I remember there were gulab jamuns, pedas and rasmalai after dinner, and I with my passion for sweets and without my mother's eagle eye on me, rapidly consumed a meal composed entirely of sweets. Then, overcome by the weight of my pimples, my oily skin, lanky hair and my intense shyness, I went to our bedroom and slept.

Now, twenty years later, I try and imagine what would have happened had my sister told my parents about the rape. They would, of course, have called it off. And Sangeeta, with her lost virginity would have continued to live with our parents, a fallen woman, as people would say. Despoiled, she would have faded quietly away into the greyness of eternal spinsterhood, while my parents prayed that some nice man would come along and love her in spite of it all, not questing the unbroken hymen. Had I been older, I would have told my parents and watched them shrivel away with barely a rustle, accepting this as their karma for sins committed in their last births, cradling their first-born, bearing forever the burden of an unmarried and deflowered daughter. And the people, oh the people would have talked and talked and the fault would have been entirely hers.

And what of Nikhil, the groom-to-be? Twenty-five to Sangeeta's twenty, he was a man so tall, so attractive, so charming, that he put to shame Darcy, Rochester and almost, but not quite, Rhett Butler. Theirs was an arranged marriage and as is inevitably the case, they fell violently in love. What romance! What courtship! What a profusion of roses for Sangeeta, what an exchange of love letters! Though they lived in the same city, they wrote to each other every day, went out with parental approval every other day.

A romantic though I was, I could not imagine what they could write about after meeting so often. Didn't they talk? If I received vicarious pleasure from my books, it was nothing to that which I received from their romance. But, consumed by shyness, I could barely talk to Nikhil or his brother Abhinay who was Sangeeta's age and almost as handsome as Nikhil. Their parents were kind to me. They would pat my head and declare that I was a polite and good girl. Which was true, for being shy, I could be nothing if not good and polite. Besides, what else could they say about me? I had neither looks nor charm nor poise. Sangeeta had all three. She made me giggle with her chatter, let me use her old lipsticks, feel her silk sarees. She cooked me my favourite dishes, told me stories about the excitement and adventure in her world – the grown-up world. She bought me books, usually ones I had long outgrown, but it didn't matter. She was wildly extravagant and almost always happy. She believed that money was meant to be spent and life was meant to be enjoyed, and she did both with abandon. When she was at home I didn't mind not reading; instead I watched her and listened to her. I thought her the most beautiful woman I had ever seen and her eyes were always brimming with laughter. Unlike mine which were always sad and lost, God knows why, for then I had nothing to be sad about.

That night Sangeeta and I put each other to sleep. I don't think she slept, but I did, deeply, the sleep of the young. When I awoke she was locking her six suitcases.

And so they were married late that night, on the auspicious time the pandit had augured. The pandit chanted the shlokas that nobody understood and my sister and Nikhil, under a mandap decorated with marigolds and surrounded by matkas painted green and red and white, went seven times around the holy fire. Abhinay was sitting behind Nikhil, I behind Sangeeta, and, as I cried, Abhinay patted my hand. I found myself holding his finger and bending it back and I think I would have broken it if he hadn't, in shock and pain, snatched it away. No one noticed and I continued sobbing with all the other weeping women.

The day after the wedding, Sangeeta and Nikhil came home, she in a green Kanchivaram saree with a magenta border, ruby drops in her ears, he in a spotless white silk pyjama-kurta. 'Made for each other', as the cigarette ad said, and I thought, 'It's all right, it's all

94

right now,' relief washing over me in waves. Then I saw her eyes, blank, listless. We all sat in the puja room and my mother performed a short puja. After it was over we ate and as my parents talked to Nikhil, my sister took me to the bedroom, sat on the bed, sat me at her feet, and, looking away from me at the wall, began to talk, her voice flat, expressionless, compulsive. Nikhil hadn't done anything last night. She had recoiled and he had attributed it to natural shyness and apprehension. He had soothed her forehead and said, take your time. And she, shivering with distaste, lay awake all night. Nikhil sickened her, nauseated her. 'Didi,' I said, 'Didi, please don't.' Still looking away from me, Sangeeta said, 'Do you know what Abhinay did?' 'No,' I said, rising, but she pushed me back to the floor, then described at length the rape and I listened, nausea rising, till the very end when I saw her lying bleeding on the cool floor. Then my mother came into the room, Sangeeta's expression changed to the sister I knew and she hugged me.

The following month Abhinay moved in with them. He needed coaching for his chartered accountancy exams and Nikhil, being a chartered accountant, would coach him. Their mother was pleased and fondly said that now Abhinay had a bhabi who would cook and look after him. When my sister told us this at her next visit, my mother's face grew grim with disapproval. It was unhealthy, she told my father after Sangeeta left. When Nikhil went to work Sangeeta and Abhinay would be together all day – it was unhealthy. My father, disturbed, cleared his throat.

Fear for my sister, coupled with guilt at my own behaviour, engulfed me. I had avoided being alone with her on the occasions she came home and refused to visit her in her house with my parents. When she came home I would sit in the living-room with everyone else, ignoring Sangeeta's plea that I should show her my books. Now, terrified at the new development, I went to the nearby temple and prayed. I told the Gods that if they made things all right for my sister I would never marry, sacrifice forever my Rochester-like husband. Not enough, not enough. I prayed that if things had to change, and in order to effect the change if I had to sacrifice what I most loved, I would sacrifice books, not all books (I was still in school), but fiction. I would stop reading fiction now, today. I prostrated myself before Ganesh, Lakshmi, Saraswati and Hanuman, and having appeased them all with coconuts, I came home.

Time stopped. Not being able to read, there was nothing to do. School was closed for the summer holiday and my only friend had gone to visit her grandparents. By the next evening I was in a ferment of boredom. I could not live without my books but I could not break my vow to the Gods. What to do? I finished a box of sweets in the fridge, stared hungrily at *Jane Eyre* which I had been reading for the third time (why hadn't I finished it before making my vow?) and fantasised about spending a day in the library. I stood for a long time before the bookshelf in my bedroom, closed my eyes, took out a book at random and opening it, smelled it deeply, the smell that still makes my stomach tighten with excitement and anticipation. Smelling wasn't breaking a vow. Then I thrust the book back. I took a walk to the nearby library, assured myself that I had read most of the books and that none were worth re-reading. Craving, tearful, I walked back home. There my father presented me with a heavy cardboard box. I opened it. Books, books, books. 'All second-hand,' my father said happily. 'I couldn't resist the bargain for my little girl.' 'But,' said my mother the disciplinarian, 'One at a time, *not* more than *one* a day, or else you'll get mental indigestion. Choose one,' she told me, 'and you lock the rest away,' she told my father. She knew too well my ability to drug myself with books and prescribed as low a dose as she possibly could, irritated by my state of stupor during my reading spells.

Watery-eyed, I looked away and said, 'No, I don't want to read, I've outgrown books.'

'You're learning to be sarcastic, aren't you?' my mother retorted. 'Talking this way won't get you more than one.'

'Don't want any,' I said and went to my bedroom, bereft, broken. My father followed me and sat beside me apprehensively. 'Are you unwell? Do you miss your sister?'

My sister. My sister. I had forgotten my sister. My sister. I began to wail and miraculously, Sangeeta entered the room. I caught hold of her saree palla. 'Come back home,' I cried, 'don't go back. Come back home.' I pulled her palla till the saree tore at her shoulders, screaming, 'I won't let you go back, I won't let you go back.' My mother, books forgotten, rocked me in her arms. Then Sangeeta cradled me in hers, whispering in my ear, 'If you tell anyone I'll deny it, I'll never talk to you, I'm finished.'

When I finally emerged from the room, a confused Nikhil patted me awkwardly and gave me a chocolate. Dinner was a quiet affair; my parents still shocked by my unprecedented behaviour. I went to bed immediately after dinner. Sangeeta followed me and sat on the bed. 'No,' I said, 'Didi, no.' Her head turned away from me, she told me that every morning when Nikhil was away on work, Abhinay raped her and at night Nikhil did.

'No, didi, don't.'

'Abhinay does it every single day. And, at night, after coaching him for his exams, Nikhil does the same thing. Only, Nikhil takes ten times as long because he thinks he's being patient, but it always hurts me, always, it doesn't matter how you do it . . . it's the same thing. Nikhil's patience only prolongs the pain, I detest them, I . . .'

I put my fingers in my ears. Sangeeta turned to me and removed them. She held both her hands over mine and hissed, 'Listen, *listen.*' Then, still holding my hands, she continued, 'Nikhil thinks I've changed. He says I've lost my spontaneity, my warmth, lost it all, all of it. He doesn't understand me, he says.' And she became quiet, and almost wistful. I got out of bed and went to the living-room.

After they left I asked my mother how long one had to sacrifice something to the Gods in order for one's wish to be fulfilled. 'At least a year,' she said, then sighed, 'and sometimes, never.' My mother kept innumerable fasts and was forever giving up sweets or meat or something she loved as part of the many bargains she struck with God. If never, I asked, why didn't she stop? 'How can I?' she answered. 'After all these years.'

And so I took *Jane Eyre* and ravenously finished it for the third time. I asked my father for the books he had got for me, and frenzied, finished fourteen in a week. 'It's the summer holiday, so do what you want,' my mother snapped in exasperation.

Sangeeta came home on three occasions after that, each time in a saree brighter than the last, and each time I sat glued in my chair in the living-room with the rest of the family, ignoring her pleas to talk in the bedroom. 'Bad girl,' she said once, pouting. 'You don't love your sister.' My mother said, 'Go and talk to your sister, you don't have to sit with us.' I burst into tears. 'Everyone bosses me around,' I said inadequately. And Nikhil, dear Nikhil produced a chocolate, and, giving it to me, said, 'For heaven's sake, let her be'. I could see unhappiness writ large on his face and when I caught him looking at my sister, he looked bewildered. She talked non-stop when she came home, her hands moving, bangles tinkling and she wouldn't listen to anyone else. My parents obviously found nothing wrong and my mother once commented that she had become even more talkative after her marriage.

Then for some time, I think two weeks, Sangeeta didn't come home. One night I woke up screaming in my sleep, emerging from a nightmare where the sound of the shehenai mingled with the sound of Sangeeta moaning and I saw her covered with marigolds and Nikhil and Abhinay on either side of my dead sister. I woke to find my parents bending over me and in anguish I called out my sister's name. 'Didi's dead,' I told my parents. 'Didi's dead.' My mother held me as my body was racked with sobs and my father in his striped pyjamas looked bewildered.

The next morning my parents called my mother's youngest sister home for lunch. Mala Mousi was a gynaecologist and my parents no doubt attributed my hysteria to some vague, ill-defined, ill-articulated problem, thought perhaps that my hormones were going awry, my periods on their way, imagined that in some obscure fashion I was jealous of my sister's fairy-tale marriage, wished her dead, that beneath my quiet exterior lay suppressed violence and anger. They had seen the change occurring after Sangeeta's marriage and, typically, refused to question me on matters so explosive, and handed me over to Mala Mousi. At thirty, Mala Mousi was twelve years younger than my mother. She was slim, attractive with pert, sharp features and short, dark hair, direct brown eyes and a nose so small and straight that I almost died of envy every time I saw it. She was brisk, sharp and cutting and everyone including my mother was a little scared of her. Sangeeta found her most intimidating – too direct, too crisp, too outspoken, too independent. Mala Mousi, she felt, had too many sharp edges and not enough of the softness and oozing affection she associated with our Aunts. She found Mala Mousi's remarks too penetrating, her views shocking and her attitude to the world too serious to justify a life that was meant to be enjoyed. 'She thinks too much,' Sangeeta would tell our mother. 'There's no point philosophising on life and all that rubbish. She doesn't know how to have fun. And what's the point of all her philosophy and reading if she still isn't married?' For Mala Mousi at thirty was single and, to my horror and admiration, seemed none the worse for it. Mala Mousi did love life, but her love for life was of a different nature from Sangeeta's. It was serious, contemplative, silent. I found her optimism impossible to understand in the light of her two broken engagements, her constant fighting for her privacy and independence, the fact that she lived alone and that her family pitied her unmarried state and constantly reminded her of it. None of this seemed to affect Mala Mousi, who was quite ruthless with her six sisters and reminded them at regular intervals that she was the only one who wasn't using her education to cook. I could share my love of books with her since she too was a voracious reader. She listened to me quite seriously, never babied me, and on my questioning, was perfectly willing to talk to me about issues like God and the universe and what we were doing in it. She told me that she didn't believe in God and certainly not in Heaven and Hell, a revelation I tried hard to swallow with equanimity. According to her Heaven and Hell only existed on earth and as hard as I tried, I could never figure this out. In the convent where I studied, Heaven and Hell were realities you could not ignore, and I was sure Purgatory was the place for me, since I sinned by reading books that were forbidden. In school we had our Christian God, at home our Hindu ones, and I had no trouble in believing in both. When the nuns told us about the miracles Christ performed, I would chime in with the miracles Krishna performed, for I truly loved them both, and the nuns would listen, patient, amused, disbelieving. I loved the Bible almost as much as I loved the *Ramayana* and the *Mahabharata*, for they were all stories that stirred me deeply, moved me to inevitable tears. I wept when Lord Rama abandoned his pregnant wife in the forest. Unfair, unjust. All because he had overheard a conversation where one of his subjects questioned Sita's purity. All because Lord Rama wanted to show his subjects that he did care what they thought. And so, without telling Sita, and she pregnant, he sent his brother, Lakshmana to escort her to the forest and leave her there, alone, unprotected. '*How* could he, Ma, how *could* he?' I cried every time she told me this story. Once, my father, overhearing this, said, 'Such are the Gods we worship.' I wept too for Draupadi, gambled away by her five husbands, the Pandavas, along with their kingdom, to their enemies, the Kauravas. I wept as Duryodhana ordered Dussasana to strip Draupadi naked, as Dussasana began pulling at her saree before the entire court, and Draupadi's five husbands, helpless, watched. '*How* could they, Ma?' I cried. '*How* could her husbands do it?' And my mother told me how Draupadi vowed that one day she would wash her hair in Dussasana's blood and till then her hair would lie loose and uncombed. Then I sighed with anger and anticipation. And my father, listening again, reaffirmed his disgust with the men in our mythology. The *Ramayana* and the *Mahabharata* abounded in passion, intrigue, vengeance and retribution – stories within stories within stories, and ultimately, of course, Good always triumphed over Evil. They had to be true, I reasoned, they absolutely had to, for how could anyone possibly have the imagination to make it all up?

Mala Mousi, in addition to her apocalyptic views, also smoked, to my parents' disapproval and embarrassment. 'Decent women don't smoke,' my father would tell my mother, and my mother, torn between her assent and her love for her baby sister, would not reply. She even drank occasionally, and she did both with such grace and style that, in my bedroom, I would often go over each gesture, the elegant lift of her slim hand, the leisurely movement of her long fingers holding the cigarette, her magenta lips coolly exhaling smoke. I longed both to impress her and impress upon her that I too had views to express that were radical. But I did not. I didn't even argue with my parents, for, besides wanting to read more, there was nothing to argue about.

Yes, Mala Mousi fascinated me. But I didn't aspire to be like her because to do so would mean no marriage and no babies and I wanted both. However, not to be like her would mean to be like my mother who had marriage and babies and was fat, comforting, unexciting, exacting, loving, practical, oozing security and discontentment. And every woman I saw around me who was married was like my mother – totally, completely unromantic. Was there no in-between?

Before lunch Ma and Mala Mousi were closeted in my parents'

bedroom and many years later I was told that the conversation went something like this:

Ma: Geeti's seriously disturbed. I don't know what to do.

Mousi: Talk to her. Find out.

Ma: Perhaps she's had her periods and doesn't know what do to?

Mousi: Ask her.

Ma: You're a gynaecologist. Check her up.

Mousi: What do you mean, check her up! She's your daughter for heaven's sake, and having her periods isn't a disease. The poor child.

Ma: Mala, beti, please talk to her.

Mousi: Didi, you're being totally irresponsible. The poor child needs you, not me.

Ma: Mala, beti, I think she's seriously disturbed about Sangeeta's marriage.

Mousi: Why?

Ma; She's behaving in such a strange manner – she cries for no reason and yesterday she dreamt that Sangeeta was dead – do you think she wants her dead?

At this point my mother burst into tears. Then Mala Mousi lectured her on her repression, her stupidity, her utter blindness to my loneliness.

'But I wasn't lonely,' I tell her now, twenty years later. 'I can't recall ever having been lonely.'

'Rubbish,' Mala Mousi says. 'You were a solitary child with practically no friends. You were so lost in your world of books that the real world eluded you completely. And you were totally, horribly oblivious to the terrible burden placed on you by your selfish sister.'

'She had no one else,' I say. 'No one.'

'She had your parents,' Mala Mousi says. 'She had a choice. She chose to stay in that masochistic set-up and use you.' Suddenly her eyes fill and she murmurs, 'The poor child, poor, poor Geeti.'

I persist. 'She was terrified that no one would believe or understand. She wasn't even aware that a choice existed.' Things are so cut and dried for Mala Mousi. Mala Mousi says, 'Your beloved sister was weak. She accepted every bit of her suffering and that made her a masochist.'

But of that day, twenty years ago, Mala Mousi's lecture to my mother, the strained lunch . . . After lunch Mala Mousi asked me to tell her about the books I was reading. We went to my bedroom, and in the middle of my talk on Jane Eyre's sad childhood, I faltered.

'Something is bothering you, Geeti,' Mala Mousi said.

'No,' I replied, for if I spoke my sister would die.

'Have you had your periods?'

I blushed. 'No.'

'Do you know why women have them?'

'Oh yes,' I said airily. 'If women have periods, then they can have babies.'

'Yes,' she answered and then told me about a woman's anatomy and reproductive organs, and then about a man's. After this, to my acute embarrassment, she told me about the sexual act, mixing it nicely with biology.

When she finished I said, 'I bet you don't know how *much* it hurts.'

'Rubbish,' said my aunt.

'*I* know,' I said. '*You* don't know.'

'Actually,' Mala Mousi said, 'I don't know. Why don't you tell me?'

'You'll know when you get married,' I said sadly.

'But you're not married, Geeti. How do you know?'

'I know people who are married, Mousi, friends,' I clarified hastily.

'And what do your married friends tell you?'

'I have one married friend,' I said, 'whose brother-in-law raped her two days before the wedding.'

'And then?'

'Then her brother-in-law came to stay with them and now he rapes her in the morning and her husband rapes her at night.'

I noticed that Mala Mousi's hands were shaking. She said, 'Geeti, my child, is that woman your sister?'

I did not answer. I felt my throat was paralysed. My frightened face was answer enough. 'Don't tell Ma,' I said.

Mala Mousi took my hands in hers. 'Geeti, baby, trust me. Do you believe I'll never harm your sister?'

'Yes,' I whispered, the tears flowing.

She wiped my tears and said, 'We'll have to tell your mother and your father.'

'No.'

'Yes. They'll get your sister back home. She'll be safe. No one will harm her. They'll never let her go back. And *whatever* happens, I'll be with you.'

'Promise? Cross your heart and promise.'

'I cross my heart,' she echoed, doing it, 'and I promise.'

'Ma can't take it,' I said. 'She'll become hysterical.' Mala Mousi pressed my hand. 'But Daddy,' I said, 'will be brave and strong. He is,' I struggled for the word, 'an invulnerable man.'

For some time we sat together quietly, Mala Mousi, her arm around me, stroking my forehead. I was filled with a sense of peace and comfort I had never known before and have never known since. Then I looked up and saw that Mala Mousi, my strong, no-nonsense Mala Mousi, was crying quietly. The fear rushed back, making me dizzy and I looked at her with such terror that she covered my eyes with her wet fingers. She said, 'Nothing will happen to Sangeeta. I'm crying for you.'

I sighed deeply, then smiled. '*I'm* all right.' I looked up at her. 'See, I'm all right.'

I really believed I was.

And so Mala Mousi called my parents to my bedroom and told them. I waited for Ma's loud tears and lamentations, but there were none. She sat limply against her chair, the faint lines around her mouth suddenly darker, her large eyes unfocused. It was my father who wept, not silently and soundlessly as I believed men cried, but in spasms of uncontrolled sounds, a sight so impossible, so unbearable, that I then felt the complete and irrevocable collapse of my world.

Mala Mousi helped me pack my suitcase and then we went to her apartment to stay for a week. She told me that my parents would get my sister back home and it would be better for me to stay with her for a short time.

That evening she told me with infinite gentleness, that my sister had died in her sleep.

After the first storm of grief, I lay in her arms and said, 'She must have died of a broken heart.' They didn't let me attend the cremation and Mala Mousi didn't either, but stayed with me, holding me during my periodic bursts of weeping.

Sangeeta did not die in her sleep and of course, she did not die of a broken heart. I discovered this four years after the event, and then only because my kid cousin, an irritating girl of great precocity, wanted me to tell her a story. I, absorbed in my book, had no intention of, or interest in indulging her. So she said, 'I bet no one told you that Sangeeta didi died because she hung herself from the fan.'

I put down my book.

'I knew I could stop you reading your stupid book,' she crowed.

I stared at her.

She grinned. 'And before she killed herself she cut off Abhinay's . . . *thing* and he died bleeding.' And overcome with embarrassment at mentioning Abhinay's 'thing', she covered her mouth and giggled.

They all knew, all, all of them, our relatives, neighbours and the entire city where we had lived, and which we moved out of a month after her death. They all knew, since of course, it made headlines in the local newspapers and there were the police, the journalists and curious people like tidal waves against our door. During that entire period I was at Mala Mousi's, kept away from newspapers and people, and soon after I left with my parents for another city, a place too distant for our relatives to descend as regularly. They all knew that when my parents entered Sangeeta's house (the front door was unbolted), she was hanging from the fan, and Abhinay lay below, next to the door.

How did she do it? When he was sleeping, probably, the sleep of the satiated, the safe, knowing Nikhil was away on work for a week. After that she must have locked the bedroom door, watching and hearing him as he tried to crawl towards it, watching and hearing him collapse. In the note she left for me she wrote, 'Today

104

Abhinay raped me for the fifty-second time. I am pregnant. I can hear him dying and I like the sound.' Did she then carefully place the note on the table, and hands folded, patiently watch Abhinay die? Or did she, as he screamed, trying to crawl towards the locked door, whisper to him about the fifty-two times?

There was a bottle of Ganga water on the side table, which she' had drunk before stepping on to the chair.

It was Mala Mousi who finally told me all this. My parents, when I confronted them, were of no use. In the kitchen I held my mother and shook her, begging for the truth. My mother, leaning against the kitchen wall, shook her head, her face wet. I held her face in both my hands then, and forced her to look at me; but her eyes, streaming, looked at the ceiling. Then I went to my father who was sitting in the veranda. He had heard me. Face averted, he said hoarsely, 'Don't ask me anything.' 'Tell me,' I shrieked, 'tell me!' The next-door neighbour peeped out from her door and my cousin cowered in the corner of the veranda. Then I went to my parents' bedroom, opened my mother's saree trunk, rummaged in the folds of her sarees till I found the money carefully tucked away, my mother's only savings put away each month from the household money. I counted four hundred rupees in ten and five rupee notes. The next day I took the train to the city where Mala Mousi lived, the city we had left four years ago. My parents, unprotesting, let me go.

Mala Mousi also told me that my parents, ravaged with grief and shock, had broken down completely, and that Nikhil had looked after them for a week as a son would. Nikhil's parents, though mad with grief and remorse, accepted their son's fate as retribution. They too eventually left the city. Mala Mousi showed me some of the women's magazines that had written about Sangeeta, making the case an issue. One compared her to Draupadi on the battlefield after the war had been won by the Pandavas, washing her hair in the blood of the man who had humiliated her, fulfilling her vow like a woman possessed.

'But she was no Draupadi,' Mala Mousi tells me today, twenty years after the event. 'She had no courage, no endurance, no ability to sustain herself or others.' My aunt, so kind and compassionate with me, does not spare my sister or my mother. She tells me that my mother has been irresponsible at each stage. 'First she hands you over to me to find out what you're disturbed about, then she turns to religion after Sangeeta's death, then she refuses to tell you anything, leaving you to find out from that precocious cousin of yours.'

I defend my mother. 'You can't expect her to discuss it with any equilibrium.'

Mala Mousi grunts. 'No, I can't. So I do it for your parents both times.' She pauses. 'She lets her children find out through a series of inopportune accidents, as she herself did when she got married. One would think her own experience would sensitise her to her children, but no. Did you know that the first time your mother was in labour, she took medicine for stomach-ache?' She notes my aghast expression with satisfaction. She rubs it in. 'Sangeeta's conception was one big accidental discovery, her birth another.' Mala Mousi has virtually stopped seeing my parents. 'My sister depresses me,' she says.

'You're not one for euphemisms, Mousi,' I murmur, and she smiles reluctantly. My mother doesn't merely depress Mala Mousi, she infuriates her, enrages her. My mother is now fanatically religious, praying and meditating for six hours a day. On my visits home (and they are increasingly briefer now), I hear her bed creak at 4 every morning, listen to the sounds of her entering her bathroom, bathing, emerging and getting dressed. Then the smell of incense drifts into my room. If I arrive unexpectedly at my parents' home and she is in the middle of her prayers, she does not come out to greet me, and I sit in my bedroom and await the end of her puja, while my father, still unable to make tea, hovers around me and says I've become thin. My mother is practising detachment, believing completely that attachments only bring sorrow. When she isn't praying, she asks about my work as a surgeon and about my separation in a desultory manner, not always listening to my response. My father, always a believer of sorts, is still, strangely, one. Once in a while he shakes his head and says, 'Nothing is understandable', then follows this with, 'God has His ways'. Mala Mousi says that in the process of my mother's prayers and my father's sighs they have lost whatever little ability they had to be responsible and make decisions. She sees the whole affair as the inevitable result of their attitudes and choices, rather than the act of a God who has His ways, as my father says, or as retribution for sins committed in the last birth, as my mother believes. But for all her raving, all her intolerance, Mala Mousi is a woman of great optimism, and, therefore, I feel, of great courage. She has no complaints about a cruel fate or a malevolent God, believing, of course, in neither, accepts it when things go wrong in her life, and for the rest, goes about delivering babies, tending to her garden and reading with great zest.

Was there no in-between, I asked at twelve. Yes, there is. I am the in-between; it was only a question of time. A question of time when my nose became finer, my eyes with kajal, larger, my hair actually thicker and longer. A question of time when the pimples vanished gracefully, the breasts appeared mysteriously, the hair on my arms and legs disappeared – waxed determinedly, my eyebrows arched and distanced themselves, having been plucked painstakingly. It was only a question of time . . . a time not still and stagnant like my mother's, but one entirely my own. Time passed as I waited for the man who would be my Rochester, my Rhett Butler, my Darcy, my David, my Sanjeevani, my life-giver, my healer. I foisted all these attributes on the man I eventually married, waited for his eyes to turn dark with compassion and understanding as I told him the story of my life. Mad, obsessed, he said of me. Crazy, he said of my sister. The less he listened, the shriller I became. As I eventually turned away from him in bed, he said, it must be running in the family.

And so I went back to Mala Mousi. She listened. No questions here, no judgments. I spoke of Sangeeta, my parents, my husband, sobbed out my dreams and fantasies, my illusions and the reality. And when I stopped my outpouring, she began hers.

Yes, I am the in-between; not married, fat, discontented and accepting like my mother, or unmarried, uncompromising and independent like Mala Mousi, but separated for the time being from my uncomprehending, angry husband, having shed my old fantasies for another – that of empathy, tenderness and companionship. In my dreams I foist this on my resisting husband, unwilling to believe that he is as unlikely my Sanjeevani as I am his Gopi.

And like women possessed, Mala Mousi and I come back to Sangeeta every time we meet. Mala Mousi still hasn't got over the stricken twelve year old or the traumatised sixteen year old she looked after and counselled. When talking of it she speaks as though the child were not me but another girl in another time. She says she couldn't bear it then and can hardly bear it now. Sometimes, unconsciously, she talks of me in the third person. 'The poor child,' she tells me. 'The poor, poor child.' It is as though Mala Mousi has become twelve-year-old Geeti, recapitulating her experience for me, her thirty-two-year old friend, articulating all that the twelve year old never did. Then it is my turn, and I become Sangeeta, living every day and every night of my sister's marriage, recreating it to the last bloody day. Then, groaning, I tell Mala Mousi that perhaps I should be thankful for my husband. A statement that she promptly tears to shreds, berating me for acting out the wifely resignation epitaph of 'others have it worse'.

Mala Mousi's aphorisms, while sensible, were too practical for me, her philosophy of life – for her, solid and flourishing and protecting like a Banyan tree, was for me too frail a branch to hold. I wanted to believe my mother when she told me, 'It is all a delusion, everything. To think this is the real world, that is what leads us all astray.' Her eyes were bleak as she looked out of the kitchen window.

'Rubbish,' Mala Mousi said when I repeated this to her. 'It is your mother who is deluded.' Her expression softened as she saw my face. 'I know. It allows her to continue living.'

Caught between my longing to believe my mother and my longing for Mala Mousi's approval, I alternated between hope and guilt. How did Mala Mousi cope? Where did she get her optimism from, how could she be so cheerful about her future, all alone, always alone? And I, how could I even begin freeing myself from the past, desperately loving all that I remembered of my sister, quietly loving Mala Mousi, and even against my will loving my husband, in spite of his Rhett Butlerish, Rochesterlike qualities, seeing in his bewilderment, some hope?

And Nikhil. My chocolate-bearer, blind unwitting rapist, big, kind brother-in-law. Many years after Sangeeta's death he came to see me at Mala Mousi's house and for the first five minutes, so shocked was I at the change in him that I couldn't talk. He had greyed prematurely, had a slight stoop and had lost forever the charm that was so much part of him. He came to find out what Sangeeta had told me. All these years it had obsessed him, knowing that Sangeeta had talked to me, not knowing what she had said.

Year after year he had visited Mala Mousi but she had refused to betray my confidence. My parents had refused to let him see me. Mala Mousi had told me of his visits but not the reason for them. 'I thought it would be too hard on you,' she said defensively. Dear Mala Mousi. All these years, Nikhil told me, he had waited to talk to me. What had Sangeeta told me? Why, how had she borne it? When had it begun? So I told him and his face shrivelled. Shuddering, he said, 'I thought she was inhibited. O God, I was no better than my brother.' Looking down, he whispered, 'Now I understand.' There was a long silence, then Nikhil looked at me, his eyes crazed with pain, and said, 'I thought you would tell me that she loved me. I came feeling that hearing this I could go away bearing it at last. But this, oh Geeti, this is beyond bearing, beyond going away from.' After that he could not speak. We sat mutely for fifteen minutes, he looking blindly out of the window. Finally, when he left he said, 'I will have to pray. I will go to Amarnath next month to pray that I can atone to her in my next birth.' As he turned to walk away he said, 'Before I met you I had hope.'

I went back to the living-room and sat on the divan, shaking with the old grief. Even today it takes me by surprise, this feeling, and I'm twelve again and uncomprehending once more. Ah the promise of our next births where we can atone for the sins committed in this one, accept our suffering in this birth, believing all our pain is our karma for the sins committed in the last one. There is much to say for Hindu philosophy, for belief brings with it acceptance and hope. It denies the eternal damnation of Hell, makes explicable the inexplicable, is the only logical answer to the tormented why. By that logic, my parents, my sister, Nikhil and I must have sinned voluptuously, horribly, in our last births. I too, like Nikhil, pray; like my mother, I make promises to the Gods, but I do it surreptitiously. Mala Mousi would disown me if she knew, for she relegates the cycle of births to the same category as Heaven and Hell. I pray that Sangeeta's soul is resting, that if there is another birth, we will know each other again. What a ritual of secrecy and guilt my prayers are! There are times when I long for Mala Mousi's conviction of one life and one death and nothing before or after, long too, for her optimism and faith in herself. But if I had her conviction, I would not have her optimism, and could I then continue living, knowing that this is the end, that this is all? I pray, just in case.

Sharmaji and
the Diwali Sweets

◆

Outside his office building, Sharma soaked in the winter
sunshine. He contemplated, ah, Delhi in the winter, the
lush green trees, the riot of flowers, the warmth and
comfort of steaming tea, the taste of roasted peanuts, and poetry!
Poetry coursing through his veins like fire! Then he noticed the
six-storied, brown office building looming passionlessly before
him. Sharma shuddered. He averted his eyes, then deliberately
turned his back on it. To enter the monstrosity on such a day was
a sin . . . to work, a heinous crime. Chewing his paan, Sharma
closed his eyes in a spasm of sun-soaked ecstasy.

Someone rushed past him, turned and came back. It was Gupta.
'Sharmaji,' he extended both hands and grasped Sharma's. 'My
dear Sharmaji, congratulations on your promotion!'

Sharma shrugged his shoulders modestly. 'It is nothing.'

Gupta patted his back. 'So now you are an office assistant. When
are you giving us sweets to celebrate?'

'Soon,' replied Sharma, 'soon. Twenty-six years Gupta, twenty-
six years it has taken this company to recognise my service to
them, to acknowledge my sweat. After sucking me dry for twenty-
six years, they make me an office assistant, still a glorified clerk.
Arre, Gupta, by now I should have been an officer, not an office
assistant.' He shook his head.

'That will come. Do not worry, that will also come. Chalo,
some tea?'

They ambled to the canteen. Winter sunshine streamed into the room through the large window, over the red, chipped tea-stained tables and down the litter-filled floor. Sharma looked down with distaste at the blackened ceiling and the unwashed cups of tea and coffee. 'No one wants to work in this company,' he said, beckoning to a peon to clean their table. They ordered tea.

'One-and-a-half years ago,' Sharma told Gupta, 'they gave me a charge-sheet saying I was not doing any work, that I never came to the office on time. In one-and-a-half years they have changed their minds. These officers, they are like chameleons.'

Gupta lit a cigarette. 'You're right – there is no predicting them. Look at the time. It is 9.45 am. Everyone should be working. But there are three . . . five . . . seven . . . eleven . . . fifteen people in the canteen now. And if these officers catch anyone, they will catch us. The others will go free, but to us they will say, you are not working, you are wasting time drinking tea. We are in their bad books so they will look out only for us.'

Sharma nodded. 'When my boss, Mr Borwankar, gave me my promotion letter, he said, Sharma, you have worked very hard. Please keep it up. I said to him, Borwankar sahib, I have worked hard for twenty-six years, for twenty-six years I have been keeping it up. And when all hope is gone, you throw me this promotion like you throw a dog a bone, and expect me to be grateful. Gupta, you should have seen his face. And then I said, this is no thanks to you. All this is due to the blessings of the personnel officer, Miss Das. It is her I will thank. Then Borwankar sahib said, Sharmaji, it is I who fill in your appraisal form, not Miss Das. To this I gave a scornful laugh. Just that. A scornful laugh. It silenced him.'

Gupta nodded his approval. 'Let us go back to our departments, Sharmaji. Otherwise they will say we are not working.'

Sharma got up. 'Yes, that is all the work they have, following us like spies. For keeping track of our movements these officers get huge salaries. Then they think they can sweeten us by that measly half a kilogram of sweets they give us for Diwali. This time I hear the union is demanding one kilogram of sweets?'

'Yes,' replied Gupta. 'Adesh Singh is demanding that the management give us one kilo of sweets this Diwali.'

They parted on the third floor and Sharma walked up to the fourth floor, knocked at Miss Das' door and opened it. The smell

111

of fresh roses wafted up to him and his nose twitched happily. How clean and sparkling her room was! What an absence of papers on her desk! What a blend of golden saree with red and golden roses! Adesh Singh, the general secretary of the workers' union was sitting opposite her, his brown safari suit as lined as the frown on his forehead. He hadn't had a haircut in years, Sharma noted disapprovingly. They both looked up.

'Madam,' Sharma said at the door, 'I have disturbed you.' Then he entered and sat next to Adesh.

'Sharmaji,' said Adesh, 'If you know you are disturbing us, why have you come in? We are discussing matters that are strictly confidential.'

Sharma sat back in his chair. 'In this company, Adesh, *no* matter is confidential. Why do you continue to delude yourself? Should I tell you what you were discussing? You were discussing the Diwali sweets issue. You were telling Miss Das that this year the company should give its employees one kilo of sweets instead of half a kilo.'

'Always poking your nose into other's affairs,' Adesh said.

Miss Das smiled. 'Congratulations, Sharmaji. I'm very happy to hear about your promotion.'

Sharma smiled back sadly. 'Madam, madam. It was in your hands to promote me to an officer. Instead you promote me to an office assistant in the clerical cadre. Why, madam, do you insult me in this manner?'

'Sharmaji, listen,' Adesh burst out. 'You talk about your promotion problems later. I am here first with issues of great importance, issues that concern all the workers in this company. All right? Now you go so that I can discuss these issues with Miss Das.'

Sharma continued sitting in his chair. He patted Adesh's back. 'You talk. I will listen. I will give advice. After twenty-six years in this company you will benefit by my presence. You have been here only five years. Miss Das, please do not mind me. Please continue with your discussions.'

Miss Das said, 'Adesh?'

'All right,' Adesh said, 'he can listen. The situation, Miss Das, is this. For years this company has been giving its employees a measly half a kilo of sweets for the festival of Diwali. Half a kilo for a company that makes lakhs in profit! I ask you, do you think we workers are beggars to whom you give alms? Ask the personnel manager that. Ask *anybody* that. For years we have been stomaching this insult. For years we have been saying, we will wait for the company to give us one kilo of sweets of its own accord. But the company will not do that. The company wants us to beg. Then only will it give us sweets, then only will it give us *anything* – increments, promotions, anything. The company wants us to crawl.' Adesh paused for breath and Sharma nodded approvingly. Then Adesh said, 'This year the workers have decided that they will not accept half a kilo of sweets. They will not be satisfied with nothing less than one kilo.'

'Adesh,' Miss Das said, 'must even sweets become an issue? Must this gift that the company gives on a festival become a demand? Sweets are not a *right* that you can demand more of. It is merely a gesture of goodwill on a festival from the company's side. Why such contention? Why such anger? I do not understand this.'

'Madam,' Adesh said, 'as a personnel officer, *you* do not understand this? This is very ironic. If *you* do not understand, then to whom should we workers go? Tell me, where should I go? Should I go directly to the general manager? Then the general manager will say, why didn't you first go to the personnel officer? And I will say, sir, she doesn't understand our problems. And then the general manager will throw me out of his heated office into the cold corridors outside.'

'I ask you,' said Sharma, 'why do only managers have heaters in their offices? Do we workers not feel the cold?'

'Why should workers feel the cold?' replied Adesh. 'Workers are not human beings.'

Miss Das took a deep breath. Sharma said, 'Arre, Adesh, calm down. If Miss Das does not understand, it is because in her innocence she cannot see. All around her is corruption. All around her is deviousness. What does she know of such things? Miss Das, we shall have to *make* you see. We shall have to disillusion you, we shall have – '

'Oh, keep quiet, you,' Adesh snapped. 'This is no time for your philosophy. Diwali is ten days away and you spout philosophy. Once the euphoria of your promotion goes away, you will come down to earth. Well, Miss Das, what do you say? When will you give us an answer?'

'Adesh,' Miss Das said, 'it is unlikely that the management will accede to a demand like this.'

'Madam, you tell me one thing. Are you, or are you not going to take this up before the personnel manager?'

'Yes, Adesh, I will. Now stop looking so angry.'

Adesh ran his fingers through his hair in a wild gesture. 'It is not easy, being the general secretary of the workers' union. No, it is not easy. The management will not give you a straight answer. Never yes, never no. Always, we shall see, we can't say, wait for some time. You put us off like you put off children, thinking we will forget. Oh, madam, we know the management's tactics. I ask you, the personnel officer. You say, you will see. You see the personnel manager. He says he will see. He asks the general manager and the general manager says no. Then the personnel manager tells you no. And you tell me, maybe next year. And from the other end the workers catch hold of me and say, fine general secretary you are, can't even get us sweets for Diwali.'

'Any demand that is reasonable will be considered,' Miss Das said, rubbing her forehead with her thumb.

Adesh gave a short laugh. 'Reasonable! What is reasonable for us workers is always unreasonable for the management. What is reasonable for the management is always unreasonable for the workers. And so we go in circles, always in circles. Diwali is a happy occasion, an occasion for celebration, and even *then*, the management cannot afford a few thousand rupees for a few extra sweets. Hah!'

'Miss Das,' Sharma said, 'you in your innocence do not under-stand the crookedness of the management. Eight years ago, they gave all the employees one kilo of sweets. Just once. They set a precedent. And you as a personnel officer know that no precedent can be changed without first consulting the workers. But at that time we did not have a union and could not bargain with the management. Now we have a union. Now the management cannot sit complacently, thinking, we can twist the workers' hands. No, madam, the time has come to twist the management's hands.'

'Well, I'll speak to the personnel manager,' Miss Das said, 'and get back to you later today.'

'Speak with conviction,' Adesh advised. 'Speak with sincerity. Speak as though you believe in us, Miss Das.'

'All right, Adesh. Now, would you both like some tea?'

They agreed readily. Miss Das ordered tea and biscuits and Adesh grew calmer, almost genial. By the time he left he had assured Miss Das of his good intentions and seemed convinced of hers.

After Adesh left, Sharma leaned forward. 'Do not mind him, Miss Das. He is distressed these days.'

'Why so, Sharmaji?'

'What can I say, madam, what can I say?'

She was silent. Sharma looked at her eagerly. Then he said, 'Yes, Adesh Singh is deeply, deeply distressed.'

'That is unfortunate,' Miss Das said.

Sharma drew his chair closer. 'There is a woman.'

'A woman?'

Sharma whispered, 'He is pursuing a woman in this office.'

'I thought he was married.'

'Exactly. That is why he is distressed.'

'I see.'

'Madam, nobody has morals these days. Least of all officers.'

'Sharmaji!'

'Madam, you are too innocent. You think everyone is like you. You think your fellow officers are good men? I know them. I know them very well. That new administrative officer, Mr Khanna. Madam, he is a dangerous man.'

'What do you mean, Sharmaji?'

Sharma drew his chair still closer to the desk and whispered, 'Mr Khanna calls our girls to his room on any pretext and talks to them. He plies them with Campa Cola and biscuits. And he keeps looking at them in a very, oh, madam, in a very *bad* manner. Madam, he has no work with our girls. Then why does he call them to his room? And all the money he spends on them he bills to the company. Madam, you officers say that we workers create problems. But the root of these problems is such officers who have a loose moral character. Madam, you are silent. I know why you are silent. You are silent because you agree with me. Even you have observed Mr Khanna's behaviour. I myself have seen how often Mr Khanna's workers come to your office, complaining

115

about his rude behaviour. It is true. He is a rude and ill behaved man. You know what he told me yesterday? He said, Sharmaji, all you do is drink tea and eat paan. Madam, if all I do is drink tea and eat paan, what business is it of his? He is not my manager. He is not the personnel officer. He does not have the authority to say such things to me.'

'Ignore him, Sharmaji. But since you say the personnel officer *does* have the authority, may I ask what work you have done this morning?'

Sharma smiled indulgently. 'Oh, madam, you are a clever one. Always you get to the point. Yes, you are an astute personnel officer.'

'Well, Sharmaji, how is your work going?'

'Extremely well, madam, extremely well. In the last few days I have filled in one whole ledger of entries of material coming into the purchase department, filed five files, placed orders for the winter uniforms for peons and sweepers, and placed orders for stationery.'

'And today, Sharmaji?'

'Today, yesterday, tomorrow, what does it matter, madam? The work has to go on and the work goes on. Like machines we go on.'

'Sharmaji, it is 11 am. Did you report to your office this morning?'

'Where, madam, how? I have been with you all morning.'

'Sharmaji! You came in here at 10 am.'

'Madam, madam, you are a very zealous personnel officer. Good. Very good. I will see you tomorrow then, with sweets to celebrate my promotion.'

Sharma sailed out and entered the large room next to Miss Das' office where the rest of the personnel department worked. Even this room, with its eight workers, was cleaner than his in the purchase department, he noted gloomily. Miss Das and her daily inspections, no doubt. He had heard that she would run her finger over the desks and shelves, and if there was dust – God help the poor peon whose turn it was to do that week's dusting. Sharma strolled over to the window across the room and wistfully gazed out into the beautiful winter morning. Was this the time to work? No, this was the time to sit on the lawns at Connaught Place, with

a cigarette, some peanuts, a paan, and contemplate. Yes, this was
a fit morning for contemplation.

'Congratulations, Sharmaji,' the clerk, Mahesh said, from
behind him, his thin, normally anxious face, now smiling.

Sharma turned. 'Thank you, Mahesh. But my promotion is no
thanks to you.'

'What are you saying, Sharmaji!'

'Mahesh,' Sharma said, wagging his finger at him, 'you have
caused me great pain. Yes, you and your attendance register which
you show Miss Das every day, saying, today Sharma is late, today
Sharma is absent, Sharma does no work. You and your precious
attendance register have pursued me like hounds for the last five
years. That Sharma is older than you is of no concern to you. That
Sharma has been in this company twenty years longer than you is
nothing to think about. But now that Sharma is promoted and is
senior to you, you want to sweet talk him, do you?'

'Sharmaji,' Mahesh said, folding his hands, 'forgive me for
having congratulated you. And forgive me also, for having done
my duty.'

'Forgiven,' Sharma said magnanimously. 'And now, maybe you
will accompany me to the canteen to celebrate my promotion over
a cup of tea?'

Mahesh hesitated.

Sharma shrugged his shoulders 'All right. You need not come.
I am a foolish and sentimental man. I thought, maybe even Mahesh
is happy about my promotion. He will celebrate with me over a
cup of tea. I was wrong. What foolishness.'

'Oh, Sharmaji, all right, I will join you for a cup of tea.'

The canteen was full, the air heavy with the smell of fried bread
pakodas. Behind the counter the peons poured tea and smoked
beedis. 'Note who all are here,' Sharma told Mahesh, 'and do not
complain to Miss Das that only I do not work.' Mahesh adjusted
his spectacles and cleared his throat. Sharma ordered tea and bread
pakodas. Then he read out two of his poems to Mahesh. Mahesh
admired them. Sharma asked him how his work was going on.
Well, Mahesh replied. 'You maintain the personal files of all the
clerks and workers, don't you?' Sharma asked casually. Mahesh
stiffened. 'Yes.'

'Who all have got increments this year?'

'That information, Sharmaji, is confidential.'

'I have heard that Adesh Singh has got a warning letter for being rude to his boss?'

'Sharmaji, do not pump me.'

'Yes, he has got a warning letter. Was his annual increment withheld?'

'Sharmaji, don't ask me these questions.'

'Yes, his annual increment has been withheld. Arre, Mahesh, why are you so secretive? Nothing remains confidential in the personnel department.'

Mahesh got up. 'Sharmaji, I had better get back to my department. There is just one hour left before lunch.'

Fifteen minutes later, Mohan, the peon from the personnel department tripped into the canteen, hailing Sharma, a wide, paan-stained grin stretching across his cheerful, unshaven face, his blue uniform flopping happily at its torn edges. Sharma greeted him joyfully and ordered two more cups of tea and more pakodas. Mohan was a good man, Sharma said, a conscientious peon. Mohan wriggled with embarrassment and delight. 'I have heard,' Sharma said, 'that no one files papers better than you.' Mohan agreed. That was a fact.

'It is unfortunate that Adesh Singh's annual increment has been withheld,' Sharma said sadly.

'It has not been withheld,' Mohan replied. 'He has just got a warning letter.'

'Who all have got special increments in this office?'

Mohan told him.

'None of them deserve it,' Sharma said. 'You, the most hard-working of peons, haven't got one.'

'Yes,' Mohan said gloomily. 'No one appreciates me.'

'*I* appreciate you, Mohan,' Sharma said. 'I will put in a word for you to Miss Das.'

'Very good of you, Sharmaji,' Mohan said, grinning.

The siren went off.

'Lunchtime,' Sharma said, happily. 'Come, Mohan, let us go and have aloo parathas at the dhaba.'

The dhaba was full of their office employees and, with some difficulty, Sharma and Mohan squeezed themselves next to some people on one of the four wooden benches. Six parathas were being cooked simultaneously above the fire, next to which, Bhaiyya, the dhabawalla squatted, turning them with practised dexterity. On the other fire a large cauldron of tea was brewing and two chotus scurried between the parathas and the paratha eaters, serving them briskly. Sharma and Mohan ate and talked. Mohan told Sharma that all Mr Khanna's workers were complaining to Miss Das about his rudeness. Mr Khanna had been overheard saying that Miss Das interfered too much. Adesh Singh was having an affair with Champa, one of the operators at the assembly line. After 5.30 pm every day, they went to the park and did God knows what. And he with a wife and two small children! And Sharmaji's boss, Mr Borwankar, was very unhappy. Mohan had heard this from Harish who worked for Borwankar sahib. Borwankar sahib had given six warning letters to the clerks in the purchase department for not working properly. Now the clerks were working even less. Borwankar sahib was going around like a thunder cloud. Mohan had overheard him telling Miss Das that he didn't know what to do and asking her how far the workers were protected by the Factory Act.

Had he, asked Sharma casually, ever heard Borwankar sahib or Miss Das discussing him? Mohan shook his head. Miss Das never discussed anyone when there was a third person in the room. But yes, he had heard Borwankar sahib grumbling to another officer about Sharmaji. They thought that if they spoke English, he, Mohan, wouldn't understand. Borwankar sahib had been saying that he hoped that the promotion would at least act as an incentive to Sharma.

They finished their lunch. 'You are a good, hard-working, sincere man,' Sharma told Mohan as they walked back to the building. 'I will give you an imported pant piece and imported cigarettes. Remember, I am in the purchase department. Anytime you want something, just ask me.'

'Sharmaji, you are very kind to a poor peon. Can you get me a cassette player?'

'Mohan, do not be greedy. No, I cannot.'

'All right, Sharmaji. You will get me the pant piece tomorrow?'

'Next week.'

Back in the building, Sharma chewed a paan and silently debated. Then he strolled to Miss Das' office, knocked and entered.

Four sweepers were in her room, all complaining loudly. They were tired of their boss, Mr Khanna. He was a slave-driver. He said they did no work. He called them names, refused to give them leave.

'Sharmaji,' Miss Das said, 'could you please come back later?'

'Poor Miss Das,' Sharma said fondly. 'Poor personnel officer.' He entered the room and sat opposite her. 'Don't trouble her,' he ordered the sweepers. 'Have patience and all will be well.'

'Sharmaji,' Miss Das said, 'please.'

'Sharmaji,' one of the sweepers said, 'we are bowed down with worries. On the one hand our boss Khannaji tells us that we should always wear our uniforms to work. On the other hand, you, who order our uniforms every year, still have not got us our uniforms this year. You people in the purchase department do no work.'

Miss Das said, 'Your uniforms are coming next week. Right, Sharmaji?'

Sharma looked worried. 'Of course, madam, of course.'

'And get us good quality uniforms,' another sweeper said to Sharma. 'You people in the purchase department have made enough money on this uniform business.'

'Quiet,' Sharma said wrathfully.

There was a knock at the door and Adesh Singh entered. 'Well, madam,' he said frowning, 'What did the personnel manager say?'

'Will the rest of you please come back later?' Miss Das said.

Muttering, the sweepers left. Sharma continued sitting. Miss Das looked at him pointedly. Adesh said, 'Oh, let him be.'

'The answer,' Miss Das said, 'is no. You will receive half a kilogram of sweets this Diwali.'

'Unacceptable!'

'In that case, Adesh, there will be no sweets distributed at all.'

Adesh arose, his eyes flashing. Sharma hit his forehead with his hand. Adesh burst out, 'Straight away you say no. No. Without thinking, you say no. The company isn't even prepared to *negotiate*. It isn't prepared to *think* about the matter. Straight away, no!'

Miss Das said, 'Adesh, you told me that you were tired of not getting direct answers, tired of going around in circles. So here *is* your direct answer – no.'

'Clever,' Adesh said grimly. '*Very* clever. All right, madam, as you wish. You have given us your direct answer. Now soon, we will give you ours.' He stormed out of the room.

'Yes, Sharmaji,' Miss Das said, tapping her pencil on the desk. 'What can I do for you?'

Sharma reached over, took the pencil from her hand and placed it on the desk. 'Less anger, madam, less anger. Anger is destructive. Anger is poisonous. Anger is blinding.'

'Have you come to talk about another problem?'

'I, madam,' Sharma said sadly, 'never talk about my problems. Everything remains here, imprisoned inside my heart. I see you are troubled. Why should I add to your troubles with my own? Yes, of course I have problems. Who will not have problems after twenty-six years in this company? Let that be. What I wish to tell you, madam, is that this decision is a dangerous one. The workers will be stirred up. There will be trouble, much trouble.'

'When the trouble comes, then we will see. Now, Sharmaji, if you'll excuse me.'

Sharma shook his head and sighed.

Strolling around the corridors, offices and production floors that afternoon, Sharma discovered that trouble was brewing, and brewing rapidly. The workers had decided on a tools-down strike. It was well timed because some important Americans were coming to see the factory that afternoon, the very same Americans with whom the company was to sign a contract. As Adesh Singh succinctly put it, 'No sweets – no work. No work – no contract.' There was an atmosphere of suppressed excitement on the production floors. The workers had never had a strike before, but then, Adesh said, curling his lips, they had never had a union before. By the time Sharma had taken a complete round of the production floors, the strike had begun. The girls were sitting at the assembly line, knitting, the men, gossiping. The supervisors sat, tight-lipped, at the end of the tables. Adesh was in the canteen, contemptuously smoking a cigarette. The sweepers squatted there too, smoking beedis, their brooms thrown aside in the corner. Word was that Miss Das was closeted with the personnel manager and the manufacturing manager. 'Now,' Adesh said to Sharma, 'these people will learn the meaning of the word, negotiation. The Americans are coming at 3.30, an hour from now. Let us see if they still want to sign a contract with a company whose workers do not work.'

'Having fun, aren't you?' Sharma questioned genially.

'Fun?' Adesh retorted. 'All this is for the cause. You think I enjoy this?'

'Everyone is enjoying this,' Sharma replied.

Adesh looked at him suspiciously. Just then Mohan entered the canteen. 'There you are, Adesh. Miss Das is calling you.'

Adesh smiled slowly. 'Tell her I will come after I finish my work.'

He lit another cigarette, finished it at leisure, and drank another cup of tea. Then he got up.

'I will come with you,' Sharma said.

'As you wish,' Adesh replied. 'She seems to have a soft corner for you.'

They entered Miss Das' room and sat opposite her.

'Adesh,' she said, 'why have the workers stopped working?'

Adesh looked at her in surprise. 'What are you saying!'

'Adesh, please stop acting. You know very well what is going on.'

'Madam I know nothing.'

'Do you know how serious it is to instigate a strike?'

'Madam, I have instigated *nothing*. I merely told my fellow workers that they would get no sweets for Diwali. If they then chose to express their disappointment, what fault is it of mine?'

'Do you realise,' Miss Das said slowly, 'the implications of going on strike without first giving notice to the management?'

'Implications?'

'The strike is illegal. Workers are liable to be dismissed.'

'*I* see,' Adesh said. 'Well, madam, then dismiss us all. There are three hundred workers in this place. Maybe you will now order your clerk, Mahesh to type out three hundred letters of termination?'

'Madam,' Sharma said, 'it is only a question of one kilo of sweets. The management is making a mountain out of a molehill.'

'We don't want your sweets,' Adesh said scornfully. 'We are not beggars.'

'Adesh,' Miss Das said, 'may I request you to tell the workers to get back to work? Tomorrow we will discuss the matter of sweets.'

'What is there to discuss, madam?' Adesh said. 'You gave us your direct answer – no. And we have accepted your direct answer.'

'We can,' said Miss Das, as though she could barely get the words out, 'we can negotiate tomorrow, as you had suggested.'

'What is the point of negotiating?' Adesh said with relish. 'Sweets are not a matter for negotiation. Sweets are merely a gesture of goodwill. Why such contention, Miss Das? Why such anger? I do not understand this.'

Miss Das was silent for a long time. Adesh said, 'No, we also do not believe in negotiations. Like you, we believe in direct answers. Maybe, if you give us a different direct answer, the workers will express their joy, instead of expressing their disappointment. And when the Americans come, half an hour from now, they will see our joyful, diligent workers, and say, this is a company we feel proud to sign a contract with.'

Sharma looked at Miss Das and moved uneasily in his chair. 'Miss Das,' he said at last, 'at this stage to think is pointless.'

Miss Das played with her ring. Then she said, 'Yes. All right, Adesh, you have your direct answer. You can tell the workers that they will get one kilo of sweets for Diwali this year.'

Adesh got up. 'Thank you, madam. Now everyone will be happy.' He left.

Sharma cleared his throat. 'Madam,' he said and stopped, as she turned away, her hand hastily brushing her right eye. 'Madam?' he repeated, horrified. She got up swiftly and walked to the filing cabinet behind her desk. From the flask kept there, she poured herself a glass of water, her back turned to him. 'Madam,' Sharma whispered, stricken.

The Americans arrived, praised the factory, signed the contract and left at 4.30 pm. Sharma spent that hour chewing paan, lost in deep contemplation at his desk in the purchase department. He was effectively screened by the tall pile of files and papers on all three sides of him. Absently, Sharma took a handful of papers from the desk and dropped them in the wastepaper basket. Absently, he repeated this action, his eyes fixed dreamily ahead of him.

'That many less papers to file, what, Sharmaji!' the clerk, Rahul chuckled from behind him.

Sharma did not turn.

'No work, Sharmaji?' Rahul persisted, grinning.

'Worries, only worries,' Sharma replied. 'I cannot work in this state of mind.'

'What worries, Sharmaji?'

'Too complex for your understanding, Rahul, too complex. It is a strange world. The best cannot survive.'

'Like you, Sharmaji?' Rahul said, chuckling.

'Yes, among others. We are all caged birds.'

At 4.30 Sharma strolled down towards the canteen. In the corridor he passed Malini, one of the girls who worked at the assembly line – short, slim, pretty and an enthusiastic union member. He stopped. 'Ah, Maliniji,' he said affably.

'Yes, Sharmaji,' she replied laughing. 'Today has been a triumph for us workers.'

Sharma sighed. 'Is that what you think? Well, keep thinking that, keep thinking that. How pleasant delusions are!'

'Delusions?'

Sharma shook his head ominously. 'You know nothing.'

'What do you mean, Sharmaji?'

Sharma sighed again. 'Some people think that the victory is not yours at all.'

Malini frowned. 'Who?'

'I cannot mention names,' said Sharma and began to walk away.

Malini stood before him. 'Sharmaji,' she said, 'explain your remark.'

Sharma scratched an unshaven cheek. 'There is a person here,' he said reluctantly, 'who feels the workers' victory is his victory.' He stopped. 'I have already said too much.'

Malini put her hands on her waist. 'Oh,' she said deliberately, 'so Adesh Singh thinks this is his personal triumph, does he?'

'I never mentioned any name,' Sharma said.

'You need not,' Malini said furiously. 'That man thinks too much of himself. So he is taking all the credit for our strike, is he!'

'Maliniji,' Sharma said, 'you said it, not I.'

There was a pregnant silence. Then Sharma said, 'Some people also think you women workers are ineffective without their guidance.'

'Oohhh,' said Malini, breathing rapidly.

'Some people think that women like you and even officers like Miss Das have no contribution to make to our factory. These people say that even though more than half of our organisation consists of women, it is the men who make decisions and effect changes.'

Malini tossed a plait over her shoulder. 'I will have to deal with Adesh Singh,' she said grimly.

'I did not say it was Adesh Singh,' Sharma reminded her gently.

Malini brooded.

'Some people,' Sharma continued, 'even tell Miss Das that production targets would not be met, but for the male workers.'

'Oh,' said Malini through her teeth. 'How can Miss Das listen to such lies?'

'She does not,' Sharma replied. 'Miss Das *always* supports you women. She says everything would collapse without our girls. She says that you all are honest and diligent.'

'At least *she* knows,' Malini fumed.

'And now,' continued Sharma, 'Miss Das, our poor harassed personnel officer, who always speaks on our behalf to the management, who always supports our cause, is alone and depressed in her office, thinking that her workers do not care for her.'

'Why should she think such a thing?'

'Some people's arguments about Diwali sweets and other issues, make her think such things,' Sharma said, meaningfully.

Malini tapped her foot on the floor. 'I have to speak to Miss Das,' she said.

'Adesh Singh is also going to speak to her,' Sharma replied.

'I am going to see her *now*,' Malini said. 'I will see you later, Sharmaji.' She walked away briskly.

Slowly, Sharma smiled.

Sharma found Adesh in the canteen. 'So Sharmaji,' Adesh said, 'Like you said, the time did come to twist the management's hands.'

Sharma sighed. 'We should see Miss Das.'

Adesh agreed. 'Just forty minutes for the factory to close. Might as well. And she usually gives us tea. Chalo.'

'Maybe,' Sharma said, as they walked to the fourth floor, 'you should be less aggressive now.'

'I am never aggressive,' Adesh said. 'I merely speak my mind with conviction. I merely abide by my principles. And now that my principles have stood the great test, I no longer need to state my convictions.'

They knocked on Miss Das' door and entered. Malini was there with two other girls from the assembly line, and they turned, sarees shimmering, pink, blue and purple, bangles jangling, laughing. Sharma's eyes brightened, his heart lightened. Turning back to Miss Das, Malini said, 'Madam, don't upset yourself about these things. They come and they go. It is thanks to you that we are getting our one kilo of sweets.'

Adesh started. 'Her? It was *me*.'

Malini made a dismissive gesture. 'You? Wasn't it *we* who laid down our tools? Where were you then – smoking as usual in the canteen! You did *nothing*!'

Sharma turned away and smiled.

Stiffly, Adesh said, 'You women talk nonsense.'

'Oh, really?' Malini retorted. 'Adesh Singh, you had better force your eyes to see what's ahead of you. Of the three hundred workers in this factory, two hundred are women. If *we* had decided to continue working, what would you have done, tell me? And if Miss Das had not spoken to the management on our behalf, would we have got our one kilo of sweets?'

'But for me,' Adesh raged, 'nothing would have happened. What would you do without the general secretary of the workers' union?'

'Adesh Singh,' replied Malini, her eyes flashing, 'listen carefully. You are the general secretary of the union. You are *not* the *union*. General secretaries will come and go. Whatever we achieve, we achieve because we now stand together. In one year we are having elections. At that time don't count on winning.'

Sharma stared at her in admiration. What a woman. *What* a woman! She was Kali!

'You will stand for the elections, then?' Adesh said sarcastically.

Malini faced him directly, arms akimbo, while the two other

126

girls and Sharma, delighted, watched on. 'Yes. Yes, Adesh Singh, yes. *I* will stand for the elections next year. Is that so inconceivable?'

'She wants to be another Indira Gandhi,' Adesh said with heavy sarcasm.

'Better that than an unscrupulous Sanjay Gandhi,' Malini retorted swiftly.

'We shall see what happens next year,' muttered Adesh.

'Yes, Adesh Singh, we shall see. Maybe next year you will stop strutting around the production floors like a peacock.' She turned to Miss Das. 'Miss Das? You are looking cheerful now. Good! We like to see you smiling. We don't like to see you sad. These things come and go. There is no point thinking too much about anything.'

Sharma, rapt, said, 'Truly, this is the age for women.'

'That it is,' Malini replied. She turned on Adesh again. 'We women work when we have to work. *We* don't loaf around the building, drinking tea, smoking cigarettes and eating paan. *We* don't take credit for whatever happens. Next time you make any demands to the management, consult me. *I* would have got you your one kilo of sweets without a strike. Chalo,' she told the girls, 'Let us go. Leave poor Miss Das alone – she has had enough people sitting on her head today.'

As they were leaving, she asked Miss Das, 'One question, madam. Where did you get that beautiful saree you're wearing?'

'At the Handloom Emporium,' she replied. 'They're on sale. This is the best time to buy one if you want to.'

Adesh curled his lips.

Malini turned to him. 'No need to look like that. I have heard the things *you* men talk about – gossiping about women all the time.' She marched out and the other two followed, giggling.

Adesh snorted. 'Talk, all talk. Women just talk.'

Miss Das raised her eyebrows questioningly.

'What I mean,' Adesh said, 'is that sometimes they should talk less. They should talk with moderation, with gentleness. Like you, madam.'

Miss Das did not answer. Adesh leaned forward in a conciliatory manner. 'Madam, you are angry with me. But why be angry? I represent the workers. You represent the management. Differences will always be there. We have to find a common meeting ground. Often hot words will be exchanged. Well, that is part of the game. It is all a game.'

'Life is a game,' Sharma sighed.

'Madam,' Adesh said. '*No* one understands your position better than I do. That is because I am in the *same* position. The workers will not give me a straight answer. Likewise, the management will not give *you* a straight answer. Only *I* know how humiliating it is for you, once to say, no, and a few hours later, to say, yes. I know, madam, because I go through it every day.' He rested his head on his hand.

'Well,' said Miss Das, 'it's over now.'

Adesh hesitated, then, reluctantly said, 'If I was harsh, forgive me.'

'That is good of you, Adesh.' They smiled at each other and Adesh left.

'Well, Sharmaji,' Miss Das said, clearing her desk, 'did you do any work today?'

'Madam,' Sharma said, 'sufficient to say that my mind has been busy today. I will not bore you with details of my work. I see you are tired. I see that the day has been an eventful and trying one for you. After all this you think I will be heartless enough to talk to you about my *work*? Oh no, madam, oh no. I have concern for you, just as you have concern for me.'

Miss Das put her papers in the drawer and locked it. She looked at her watch. 'Just ten minutes for the siren,' she said. 'Would you care to read me some of your poems, Sharmaji?'

Sharma beamed. 'Madam, you flatter me.' He took out a piece of paper from his pocket and, clearing his throat, said, 'The poem I will read, madam, comes straight from my heart.' He read out, in Hindi:

> I know what the caged bird feels, alas!
> When the sun is bright on the upland slopes;
> When the wind stirs soft through the springing grass
> And the river flows like a stream of glass;
> And the first bird sings and the first bud opes,
> And the faint perfume from its chalice steals –
> I know what the caged bird feels!

Sharma's voice faltered and he stopped. Miss Das tried unsuc-
cessfully to hide her smile. 'Sharmaji! Sharmaji! *You* have written
this poem?'

'Madam?'

'I have read this poem before in English!'

'Oh madam,' Sharma said, 'how does it matter who wrote it?
The man who writes merely expresses what so many of us *feel*.
When I read this poem in the magazine, I said, here is a man from
another country, yet a man of my own heart. A man who suffers.
And in his suffering, writes words of such beauty. Madam, if *he*
had not written it, *I* would have. It is the same thing.'

The siren went off. Sharma continued to gaze fondly at Miss
Das. She closed her bag and got up. 'Sharmaji,' she said.

'Yes, madam?'

'Please report to your office at 9 am tomorrow.'

'Yes, madam, of course, madam.'

They went out together and Sharma watched her walk slowly
towards the bus stand. It was dark already, and very cold. Sharma
rubbed his hands and buried them in his coat pocket. The smell of
roasting peanuts wafted across and the sounds of chattering girls
filled the air. Sharma looked longingly at the dhaba. He could do
with a cup of tea. But no, his wife and four children would be
waiting for him. He began walking towards the bus stop.
Tomorrow then. Tomorrow would be a fit morning for
contemplation.

Her Mother

$\blacklozenge$

When she got her daughter's first letter from America, the mother had a good cry. Everything was fine, the daughter said. The plane journey was fine, her professor who met her at the airport was nice, her university was very nice, the house she shared with two American girls (nice girls) was fine, her classes were okay and her teaching was surprisingly fine. She ended the letter saying she was fine and hoping her mother and father were too. The mother let out a moan she could barely control and wept in an agony of longing and pain and frustration. Who would have dreamt that her daughter was doing a PhD in Comparative Literature, she thought, wiping her eyes with her saree palla, when all the words at her command were 'fine', 'nice', and 'okay'. Who would have imagined that she was a gold medallist from Delhi University? Who would know from the blandness of her letter, its vapidity, the monotony of its tone and the indifference of its adjectives that it came from a girl so intense and articulate? Her daughter had written promptly, as she had said she would, the mother thought, cleaning her smudged spectacles and beginning to re-read the letter. It had taken only ten days to arrive. She examined her daughter's handwriting. There seemed to be no trace of loneliness there, or discomfort, or insecurity – the writing was firm, rounded and clear. She hadn't mentioned if that over-friendly man at the airport had sat next to her on the plane. The mother hoped not. Once Indian men boarded the plane for a new country, the anonymity drove them crazy. They got drunk and made life hell for the air-hostesses and everyone else nearby, but of course, they thought they were flirting with finesse. Her daughter, for all her arguments with her parents, didn't know how to deal with such men. Most men. Her brows furrowed, the mother took out a letter-writing pad from her folder on the dining-table and began to write. Eat properly, she wrote. Have plenty of milk, cheese and cereal. Eating badly makes you age fast. That's why western women look so haggard. They might be pencil slim, but look at the lines on their faces. At thirty they start looking faded. So don't start these stupid, western dieting fads. Oil your hair every week and avoid shampoos. Chemicals ruin the hair. (You can get almond oil easily if coconut oil isn't available.) With all the hundreds of shampoos in America, American women's hair isn't a patch on Indian women's. Your grandmother had thick, black hair till the day she died.

One day, two months earlier, her daughter had cut off her long thick hair, just like that. The abruptness and sacrilege of this act still haunted the mother. That evening, when she opened the door for her daughter, her hair reached just below her ears. The daughter stood there, not looking at either her mother or father, but almost, it seemed, beyond them, her face a strange mixture of relief and defiance and anger, as her father, his face twisted, said, why, why? I like it short, she said. Fifteen years of growing it below her knees, of oiling it every week, and washing it so lovingly, the mother thought as she touched her daughter's cheek and said, you are angry with us . . . is this your revenge? Her daughter had brushed away her hand and moved past her parents, past her brother-in-law who was behind them and into her room. For the father it was as though a limb had been amputated. For days he brooded in his chair in the corner of the sitting-room, almost in mourning, avoiding even looking at her, while the mother murmured, you have perfected the art of hurting us.

Your brother-in-law has finally been allotted his three-bedroomed house, she wrote, and he moved into it last week. I think he was quite relieved to, after living with us these few months. So there he is, living all alone in that big house with two servants while your sister continues working in Bombay. Your sister says that commuting marriages are inevitable, and like you, is not interested in hearing her mother's opinion on the subject. I suppose they will go on like this for years, postponing having children, postponing being together, until one day when they're as old as your father and me, they'll have nothing to look forward to. Tell me, where would we have been without you both? Of course, you will only support your sister and your brother-in-law and their strange, selfish marriage. Perhaps that is your dream too. Nobody seems to have normal dreams any more. The mother had once dreamt of love and a large home, silk sarees and sapphires. The love she had got, but as her husband struggled in his job and the children came and as they took loans to marry off her husband's sisters, the rest she did not. In the next fifteen years she had collected a nice selection of silk sarees and jewellery for her daughters, but by that time, they showed no inclination for either. The older daughter and her husband had had a registered marriage, refused to have even a reception and did not accept so much as a handkerchief from their respective parents. And the younger one had said quite firmly before she left, that she wasn't even thinking of marriage.

The mother looked at her husband's back in the veranda. That's all he did after he came back from the office – sit in the veranda and think of his precious daughter, while she cooked and cleaned, attended to visitors and wrote to all her sisters and his sisters. Solitude to think – what a luxury! She had never thought in solitude. Her thoughts jumped to and fro and up and down and in and out as she dusted, cooked, cleaned, rearranged cupboards, polished the brass, put buttons on shirts and falls on sarees, as she sympathised with her neighbour's problems and scolded the dhobi for not putting enough starch on the sarees, as she reprimanded the milkman for watering down the milk and lit the kerosene stove because the gas had finished, as she took the dry clothes from the clothes-line and couldn't press them because the electricity had failed and realised that the cake in the oven would now never rise. The daughter was like her father, the mother thought – she too had wanted the escape of solitude, which meant, of course, that in the process she neither made her bed nor tidied up her room.

How will you look after yourself, my Rani Beti, she wrote. You have always had your mother to look after your comforts. I'm your mother and I don't mind doing all this, but some day you'll have to do it for the man you marry and how will you, when you can't even thread a needle?

But of course, her daughter didn't want marriage. She had been saying so, vehemently, the last few months. The father blamed the mother. The mother had not taught her how to cook or sew and had only encouraged her and her sister to think and act with an independence quite uncalled for in daughters. How then, he asked her, could she expect her daughters to be suddenly amenable? How could she complain that she had no grandchildren and lose herself in self-pity when it was all her doing? Sometimes the mother fought with the father when he said such things, at other times she cried or brooded. But she was not much of a brooder, and losing her temper or crying helped her cope better.

The mother lay aside her pen. She had vowed not to lecture her daughter, and there she was, filling pages of rubbish when all she wanted to do was cry out, why did you leave us in such anger? What did we not do for you? Why, why? No, she would not ask. She wasn't one to get after the poor child like that.

How far away you are, my pet, she wrote. How could you go away like that, so angry with the world? Why, my love, why? Your father says that I taught you to be so independent that all you hankered for was to get away from us. He says it's all my fault. I have heard that refrain enough in my married life. After all that I did for you, tutoring you, disciplining you, indulging you, caring for you, he says he understands you better because you are like him. And I can't even deny that because it's true. I must say it's very unfair, considering that all he did for you and your sister was give you chocolates and books. When her daughter was six, the mother recalled, the teacher had asked the class to make a sentence with the word 'good'. She had written, my father is a good man. The mother sighed as she recalled asking her, isn't your mother a good woman? And the daughter's reply, Daddy is gooder. The mother wrote, no, I don't understand – you talk like him, look like him, are as obstinate and as stupidly honest. It is as though he conceived you and gave birth to you entirely on his own. She was an ayah, the mother thought, putting her pen aside, that was all she was; she did all the dirty work and her husband got all the love.

The next day, after her husband had left for the office, the mother continued her letter. She wrote in a tinier handwriting now, squeezing as much as possible into the thin air-mail sheet. Write a longer letter to me, next time, my Rani, she wrote. Try and write as though you were talking to me. Describe the trees, the buildings, the people. Try not to be your usual perfunctory self. Let your mother experience America through your eyes. Also, before I forget, you must bathe every day, regardless of how cold it gets. People there can be quite dirty. But no, if I recall correctly, it is the English and other Europeans who hate to bathe. Your Naina Aunty, after her trip to Europe, said that they smelled all the time. Americans are almost as clean as Indians. And don't get into the dirty habit of using toilet paper, all right?

The mother blew her nose and wiped her cheek. Two years, she wrote, or even more for you to come back. I can't even begin to count the days for two years. How we worry, how we worry. Had you gone abroad with a husband, we would have been at peace, but now? If you fall ill who will look after you? You can't even make dal. You can't live on bread and cheese forever, but knowing you, you will. You will lose your complexion, your health, your hair. But why should I concern myself with your hair? You cut it off, just like that.

The mother lay her cheek on her hand and gazed at the door where her daughter had stood with her cropped hair, while she, her husband and her son-in-law stood like three figures in a tableau. The short hair made her face look even thinner. Suddenly she looked ordinary, like all the thousands of short-haired, western-looking Delhi girls one saw, all ordinarily attractive like the others, all the same. Her husband saying, why, why? his hands up in the air, then slowly, falling down at his sides, her son-in-law, his lazy grin suddenly wiped off his face; she recalled it all, like a film in slow motion.

I always thought I understood you, she wrote, your dreams, your problems, but suddenly it seems there is nothing that I understand. No, nothing, she thought, the tiredness weighing down her eyes. She was ranting – the child could do without it. But how, how could she not think of this daughter of hers, who in the last few months had rushed from her usual, settled quietness to such unsettled stillness that it seemed the very house would begin to balloon outwards, unable to contain her straining?

Enough, she wrote. Let me give you the news before I make you angry with my grief. The day after you left, Mrs Gupta from next door dropped in to comfort me, bless her. She said she had full faith you would come back, that only boys didn't. She says a daughter will always regard her parents' home as her only home, unlike sons who attach themselves to their wives. As you know, she has four sons, all married, and all, she says, under their wives' thumbs. But it was true, the mother thought. Her own husband fell to pieces every time she visited her parents without him. When he accompanied her there he needed so much looking after that she couldn't talk to her mother, so she preferred to go without him. With her parents she felt indulged and irresponsible. Who indulged her now? And when she came back from her parents the ayah would complain that her husband could never find his clothes, slept on the bedcover, constantly misplaced his spectacles, didn't know how to get himself a glass of water and kept waiting for the postman.

With all your talk about women's rights, she wrote, you refuse to see that your father has given me none. And on top of that he says that I am a nag. If I am a nag, it is because he's made me one. And talking of women's rights, some women take it too far. Mrs Parekh is having, as the books say, a torrid affair with a married man. This man's wife is presently with her parents and when Mrs Parekh's husband is on tour, she spends the night with him, and comes back early in the morning to get her children ready for school. Everyone has seen her car parked outside his flat in the middle of the night. Today our ayah said, memsahib, people like us do it for money. Why do memsahibs like her do it? But of course, you will launch into a tirade of how this is none of my business and sum it up with your famous phrase, each to her own. But my child, they're both married. Surely you won't defend it? Sometimes I don't understand how your strong principles co-exist with such strange values for what society says is wrong. Each to her own, you have often told me angrily, never seeming to realise that it is never one's own when one takes such a reckless step, that entire families disintegrate, that children bear scars forever. Each to her own indeed.

Yes, she was a straightforward girl, the mother thought, and so loyal to those she loved. When the older daughter had got married five years ago, and this one was only seventeen, how staunchly she had supported her sister and brother-in-law's decision to do without all the frills of an Indian wedding. How she had later defended her sister's decision to continue with her job in Bombay, when her husband came on a transfer to Delhi. She had lost her temper with her parents for writing reproachful letters to the older daughter, and scolded them when they expressed their worry to the son-in-law, saying that as long as he was living with them, they should say nothing.

The mother was fond of her son-in-law in her own way. But deep inside she felt that he was irresponsible, uncaring and lazy. Yes, he had infinite charm, but he didn't write regularly to his wife, didn't save a paisa of his salary (he didn't even have a life insurance policy and no thoughts at all of buying a house) and instead of spending his evenings in the house as befitted a married man, went on a binge of plays and other cultural programmes, often taking her daughter with him, spending huge amounts on petrol and eating out. His wife was too practical, he told the mother, especially about money. She believed in saving, he believed in spending. She wanted security, he wanted fun. He laughed as he said this, and gave her a huge box of the most expensive barfis. The mother had to smile. She wanted him to pine for her daughter. Instead, he joked about her passion for her work and how he was waiting for the day when she would be earning twice as much as him, so that he could resign from his job and live luxuriously off her, reading, trekking and sleeping. At such times the mother couldn't even force a smile. But her younger daughter would laugh and say that his priorities were clear. And the older daughter would write and urge the mother not to hound her sister about marriage, to let her pursue her interests. The sisters supported each other, the mother thought, irritated but happy.

Yesterday, the mother wrote, we got a letter from Naina Aunty. Her friend's son, a boy of twenty-six, is doing his PhD in Stanford. He is tall, fair and very handsome. He is also supposed to be very intellectual, so don't get on your high horse. His family background is very cultured. Both his parents are lawyers. They are looking for a suitable match for him and Naina Aunty who loves you so much, immediately thought of you and mentioned to them that you are also in the States. Now, before losing your temper with me, listen properly. This is just a suggestion. We are *not* forcing you into a marriage you don't want. But you must keep an open mind. At least meet him. Rather, *he* will come to the university to meet you. Talk, go out together, see how much you like each other. *Just* meet him and try and look pleasant and smile for a change. Give your father and me the pleasure of saying, there is someone who will look after our child. If something happens to us who will look after you? I know what a romantic you are, but believe me, arranged marriages work very well. Firstly, the bride is readily accepted by the family. Now look at me. Ours was a love marriage and his parents disliked me and disapproved of our marriage because my sister had married out of the community. They thought I was fast because in those days I played tennis with other men, wore lipstick and bras. I wonder why I bore it. I should have been cold and as distant as them. But I was ingratiating and accommodating. Then your father and I had to marry off his sisters. Now in an arranged marriage you can choose not to have such liabilities. I am not materialistic, but I am not a fool either. I know you want to be economically independent, and you must be that, but it will also help if your husband isn't burdened with debts. I am not blaming your father. Responsibilities are responsibilities. But if you can help it, why begin married life with them? Now don't write back and say you're sick of my nagging. You think I am a nag because it is I who wields the stick and your father who gives those wonderful, idealistic lectures. Perhaps when you marry you will realise that fathers and husbands are two very different things. In an arranged marriage you will not be disillusioned because you will not have any illusions to begin with. That is why arranged marriages work. Of course, we will not put any pressure on you. Let us know if it is all right for the boy to meet you and I will write to Naina Aunty accordingly. Each day I pray that you will not marry an American. That would be very hard on us. Now, look at your father and me. Whatever your father's faults, infidelity isn't one of them. Now these Americans, they will divorce you at the drop of a hat. They don't know the meaning of the phrase, 'sanctity of marriage'. My love, if you marry an American and he divorces you and we are no longer in this world, what will you do?

When the milkman came early this morning, he enquired about you. I told him how far away you are. He sighed and said that it was indeed very far. I think he feels for us because he hasn't watered down the milk since you left. I'm making the most of it and setting aside lots of thick malai for butter. When the postman came, he said, how is baby? I replied, now only you will bear her news for us. He immediately asked for baksheesh. I said, nothing doing, what do you mean, baksheesh, it isn't Diwali. He replied, when I got you baby's first letter, wasn't it like Diwali? So I tipped him. Our bai has had a fight with her husband because he got drunk again and spent his entire salary gambling it away. She is in a fury and has left the house saying she won't go back to him unless he swears in the temple that he will never drink again. Your father says, hats off to her. Your father is always enraptured by other women who stand up for themselves. If I stood up for myself he would think he was betrayed.

Betrayal, betrayal, the mother mulled. His job had betrayed him, his strict father had, by a lack of tenderness betrayed him. India herself had betrayed him after Independence, and this betrayal he raved against every evening, every night. He told her that sometimes he felt glad that his daughter had left a country where brides were burnt for dowry, where everyone was corrupt, where people killed each other in the name of religion and where so many still discriminated against Harijans. At least, he said, his daughter was in a more civilised country. At this the mother got very angry. She said, in America fathers molested their own children. Wives were abused and beaten up, just like the servant classes in India. Friends raped other friends. No one looked after the old. In India, the mother said, every woman got equal pay for equal work. In America they were still fighting for it. Could America ever have a woman president? Never. Could it ever have a Black president? Never. Americans were as foolish about religion as Indians, willing to give millions to charlatans who said that the Lord had asked for the money. She was also well read, the mother told her husband, and she knew that no Indian would part with his money so easily. As for discrimination against untouchables in India – it only happened among the uneducated, whereas discrimination against Blacks was rampant even among educated Americans. Blacks were the American untouchables. The mother was now in her element. She too had read *Time* and *Newsweek*, she told her husband, and she knew that in India there had never been any question of having segregation in buses where Harijans were concerned, as was the case in America, not so long ago.

Don't rant, her husband told her, and lower your voice, I can hear you without your shrieking. The mother got into a terrible fury and the father left the room.

The mother wrote, you better give us your views about that country – you can give us a more balanced picture. Your father thinks I'm the proverbial frog in the well. Well, perhaps that is true, but he is another frog in another well and Americans are all frogs in one large, rich well. Imagine, when your Aunt was in America, several educated Americans asked her whether India had roads and if people lived in trees. They thought your Aunt had learnt all the English she knew in America.

The mother made herself a cup of tea and sipped it slowly. Her son-in-law hadn't even been at home the night her daughter had left. It upset the mother deeply. He could have offered to drive them to the airport at least, comforted them in their sorrow. But he had gone off for one of his plays and arrived a few minutes after they returned from the airport, his hair tousled, his eyes bright. He stopped briefly in the living-room where the mother and father sat quietly, at opposite ends, opened his mouth to say something, then shrugged slightly and went to his room.

Selfish, the mother thought. Thoughtless. The daughter hadn't even enquired about him when she left. Had she recognised that her fun-loving brother-in-law had not an ounce of consideration in him?

The two months before her daughter had left had been the worst. Not only had she stopped talking to her parents, but to him. It frightened the mother. One can say and do what one likes with parents, she told her silent child once, parents will take anything. Don't cold shoulder him too. If he takes a dislike to you and your moods, then you will be alienated even from your sister. Remember, marriage bonds are ultimately stronger than ties between sisters. The daughter had continued reading her book. And soon after, she had cut off her hair. Rapunzel, her brother-in-law had said once, as he watched her dry her hair in the courtyard and it fell like black silk below her knees. Rapunzel, he said again, as the mother smiled and watched her child comb it with her fingers, Rapunzel, Rapunzel, let down your hair. Oh, she won't do that, the mother had said, proud that she understood, she is too quiet and withdrawn, and her daughter had gone back to the room and the next day she had cut if off, just like that.

The mother finished her tea and continued her letter. Let me end with some advice, she wrote, and don't groan now. Firstly, keep your distance from American men. You are innocent and have no idea what men are like. Men have more physical feelings than women. I'm sure you understand. Platonic friendships between the two sexes does not exist. In America they do not even pretend that it does. There kissing is as casual as holding hands. And after that you know what happens. One thing can lead to another and the next thing we know you will bring us an American son-in-law. You know we will accept even that if we have to, but it will make us most unhappy.

Secondly, if there is an Indian association in your University, please join it. You might meet some nice Indian men there with the same interests that you have. For get-togethers there, always wear a saree and try to look pleasant. Your father doesn't believe in joining such associations, but I feel it is a must.

The mother was tired of giving advice. What changed you so much the last few months before you left, she wanted to cry, why was going abroad no longer an adventure but an escape? At the airport, when the mother hugged the daughter, she had felt with a mother's instinct that the daughter would not return.

There had been a brief period when her child had seemed suddenly happy, which was strange, considering her final exams were drawing closer. She would work late into the night and the mother would sometimes awaken at night to hear the sounds of her making coffee in the kitchen. Once, on the way to the bathroom she heard sounds of laughter in the kitchen and stepped in to see her daughter and son-in-law cooking a monstrous omelette. He had just returned from one of his late night jaunts. An omelette at 1 am, the mother grunted sleepily and the two laughed even more as the toast emerged burnt and the omelette stuck to the pan. Silly children, the mother said and went back to bed.

And then, a few weeks later, that peculiar, turbulent stillness as her daughter continued studying for her exams and stopped talking to all of them, her face pale and shadows under her eyes, emanating a tension that gripped the mother like tentacles and left the father hurt and confused. She snapped at them when they questioned her, so they stopped. I'll talk to her after her exams, the mother told herself. She even stopped having dinner with them, eating either before they all sat at the table, or much later, and then only in her room.

And that pinched look on her face . . . the mother jerked up. It was pain, not anger. Her daughter had been in pain, in pain. She was hiding something. Twelve years ago, when the child was ten, her mother had seen the same pinched, strained look on her face. The child bore her secret for three days, avoiding her parents and her sister, spending long hours in the bathroom and moving almost furtively around the house. The mother noticed that two rolls of cotton had disappeared from her dressing-table drawer and that an old bedsheet she had left in the cupboard to cut up and use as dusters, had also disappeared. On the third day she saw her daughter go to the bathroom with a suspicious lump in her shirt. She stopped her, her hands on the trembling child's arms, put her fingers into her shirt and took out a large roll of cotton. She guided the child to the bathroom, raised her skirt and pulled down her panties. The daughter watched her mother's face, her eyes filled with terror, waiting for the same terror to reflect on her face, as her mother saw the blood flowing from this unmentionable part of her body and recognised her daughter's imminent death. The mother said, my love, why didn't you tell me, and the child, seeing only compassion, knew she would live, and wept.

The omniscience of motherhood could last only so long, the mother thought, and she could no longer guess her daughter's secrets. Twelve years ago there had been the disappearing cotton and sheet, but now? The mother closed her eyes and her daughter's face swam before her, her eyes dark, that delicate nose and long plaited hair – no, no, it was gone now and she could never picture her with her new face. After her daughter had cut her hair, the mother temporarily lost her vivacity. And the daughter became uncharacteristically tidy – her room spick and span, her desk always in order, every corner dusted, even her cupboard neatly arranged. The mother's daily scoldings to her, which were equally her daily declarations of love, ceased, and she thought she would burst with sadness. So one day, when the mother saw her daughter standing

in her room, looking out of the window, a large white handkerchief held to her face, the mother said, don't cry, my love, don't
cry, and then, don't you know it's unhygienic to use someone
else's hanky, does nothing I tell you register, my Rani? And her
daughter, her face flushed, saying, it's clean, and the mother taking
it out of her hand and smelling it and snorting, clean, what
rubbish, and it isn't even your father's, it's your brother-in-law's,
it smells of him, and it did, of cigarettes and aftershave and God
knows what else and the mother had put it for a wash.

The mother's face jerked up. Her fingers' grip on the pen
loosened and her eyes dilated. Her daughter had not been crying.
Her eyes, as they turned to her mother, had that pinched look, but
they were clear as she removed the handkerchief from her nose. It
had smelled of him as she held it there and she wasn't wiping her
tears.

The mother moaned. If God was omniscient, it hadn't seemed
to hurt him. Why hadn't He denied the omniscience of motherhood? Oh, my love, the mother thought. She held her hand to
her aching throat. The tears weren't flowing now. She began to
write. Sometimes when one is troubled, she wrote, and there is
no solution for the trouble, prayer helps. It gives you the strength
to carry on. I know you don't believe in rituals, but all I'm
asking you to do is to light the lamp in the morning, light an
agarbatti, fold your hands, close your eyes and think of truth and
correct actions. That's all. Keep these items and the silver idol of
Ganesh which I put into your suitcase, in a corner in your
cupboard or on your desk. For the mother, who had prayed all
her life, prayer was like bathing or brushing her teeth or chopping
onions. She had found some strength in the patterns these created,
and sometimes, some peace. Once, when her husband reprimanded her for cooking only eight dishes for a dinner party, she
had wanted to break all the crockery in the kitchen, but after five
minutes in her corner with the Gods, she didn't break them. She
couldn't explain this to her child. She couldn't say, it's all right,
it happens; or say, you'll forget, knowing her daughter wouldn't.
If you don't come back next year, she wrote, knowing her
daughter wouldn't, I'll come and get you. She would pretend to
have a heart attack, the mother said to herself, her heart beating

very fast, her tears now falling very rapidly, holding her head in her hands, she would phone her daughter and say, I have to see you before I die, and then her daughter would come home, yes, she would come home, and she would grow her hair again.

Glossary

acha:	*O.K./indeed/I see*
agarbatti:	*incense*
Amarnath:	*a place of pilgrimage in the Himalayas*
Amma, Ammaji:	*Mother*
arre:	*an exclamation*
ayah:	*the woman servant who looks after the house and children*
bahu:	*daughter-in-law*
bai:	*the woman servant who washes and sweeps*
bak-bak:	*a term used to denote talking nonsense*
baksheesh:	*tip*
banyan:	*vest*
barfi:	*an Indian sweet*
barsati:	*a one- or two-roomed apartment at the top of the main house*
bas:	*enough*
beedi:	*a cheap cigarette made of tobacco leaf*
beta, beti:	*son, daughter*
bhabi:	*elder brother's wife*
Chachaji:	*Uncle (father's brother)*

chai:	*tea*
chalo:	*let us go*
chappatis:	*a kind of bread made out of wheat*
charpoi:	*a bed made out of jute coir*
chotus:	*little boys*
chowkidar:	*watchman*
dahi:	*curd/yogurt*
dahi vadas:	*a snack made of fried lentils soaked in yogurt*
dal:	*lentils*
dhaba:	*a makeshift structure where tea and snacks are served*
dhanda:	*business, but in this context, prostitution*
Didi:	*a term used to address an older sister*
Diwali:	*an important festival celebrated in North India*
diwan:	*a low setee with cushions*
dholak:	*two-sided drum, played by hand, usually at weddings*
DTC:	*the Delhi Transport Corporation*
Emergency:	*the State of Emergency declared in India by the then Prime Minister, Indira Gandhi, when all democratic rights were suspended and many atrocities took place*
Ganesh:	*the God of luck and prosperity*
gated:	*not allowed out of the gates*

Gita:	*part of the epic,* Mahabharata, *consisting of a philosophical conversation between Arjuna and his charioteer, Lord Krishna*
gopis:	*milkmaids, with whom Lord Krishna dallied*
gulab jamun:	*an Indian sweet*
Hai Bhagwan:	*O God*
Hai Ram:	*O Ram*
Hanuman:	*the monkey God, a great devotee of Lord Rama*
haram zada:	*a term of abuse*
Harijan:	*an untouchable*
IAS:	*the Indian Administrative Service (considered very prestigious, also a great status symbol)*
jamun:	*a purple berry eaten during the monsoons*
Ji:	*a term of respect*
jooda:	*hair tied in a bun*
kaamchor:	*one who shirks work*
kabadiwalla:	*collector of old newspapers, jars, odds and ends*
kadhai:	*a large vessel in which food is cooked*
kadhi:	*a dish made of curd*
kajal:	*kohl*
Kali:	*the Goddess symbolising female power and the destruction of evil, mostly worshipped in Bengal*
karma:	*the philosophy according to which the actions in your previous life determine your fate in this one, and your actions in this life determine your fate in the next one, and so on.*

koyal:	*the cuckoo, a bird always associated with the monsoon*
Krishna, Kannhaiyya:	*Lord Krishna*
kurta:	*a long tunic which is worn over pyjamas or trousers*
lahenga:	*a full-length Indian skirt*
Lakshmi:	*the Goddess of wealth*
lassi:	*buttermilk*
Madrasi:	*a condescending and misguided term for all South Indians, used by most North Indians*
Mahabharata:	*a great Indian epic*
malai:	*cream*
Mamaji:	*Mother's brother*
Mamiji:	*Mother's brother's wife*
mandap:	*a beautifully decorated, small structure beneath which the wedding ceremony is performed*
mangalsutra:	*a gold chain strung with black beads, only worn by married women*
maska:	*flattery*
matka:	*earthen pot*
mela:	*a fair (in this context, a gathering)*
memsahib:	*a term used to address the mistress of the house by the servants*
mousi:	*mother's sister*

MP:	*the state of Madhya Pradesh*
namaste:	*a greeting with hands folded*
nimbupani:	*a sweetened lime drink*
paan:	*betel nut*
pakodas:	*a fried snack*
palla:	*the part of the saree that comes down over the shoulder*
Pandit:	*the Brahmin who performs a wedding or other religious ceremony*
payals:	*anklets*
pedas:	*an Indian sweet*
peon:	*someone in the office who is employed to do odd jobs like getting tea, posting letters etc.*
puja:	*prayers*
puri-aloo:	*a bread made of flour and fried, with potatoes*
pyjama-kurta:	*a loose, long top and loose pants*
Radha:	*Lord Krishna's most favoured devotee*
rakshash:	*a demonic figure from Hindu mythology*
Rama:	*Lord Rama, an incarnation of Lord Vishnu*
Ramayana:	*the epic in Indian mythology about Lord Rama*
rangoli:	*a typically Indian decoration, made on the floor of houses when festivals are celebrated*
rasmalai:	*an Indian sweet*

149

Ravana:	*the man who abducted Lord Rama's wife, Sita, and against whom Rama waged a war*
Sahib:	*a term used to address someone your senior or superior (a male)*
samaj:	*a place where important occasions, like marriages and festivals are celebrated*
sangeet:	*music*
sanjeevani:	*life-giver (the plant, sanjeevani, was brought by Hanuman to bring Lord Rama's brother, Lakshmana, back to life in the war against Ravana)*
scooterwalla:	*the driver of the scooter, a three-wheeler*
Shani:	*Saturn – an unlucky star*
shehenai:	*an Indian instrument, the music of which is often played during weddings*
shlokas:	*the chants in Sanskrit during ceremonies*
sindoor:	*red powder applied to the parting of the hair, a sign of being married*
tawa:	*a flat skillet*
tiffin-carrier:	*lunch box*
UP:	*the state of Uttar Pradesh*
Yannas:	*a derogatory term used for South Indians by many North Indians*
yar:	*friend*
Youth Congress:	*the youth branch of the Congress party*